I0597480

The New Life of Angelina

Teresa Maldonado

The chapter titles of *The New Life of Angelina* are taken from the book *The Origin of Species* by Charles Darwin, and the phrases below are taken from movies and video games.

The New Life of Angelina

First Edition: 2022

ISBN: 9781524318444
ISBN eBook: 9781524328399

© of the text:
  Teresa Maldonado

© Layout, design and production of this edition: 2022 EBL

Table of Contents

Chapter 1
Fertilization of Orchids

Behind myths there is always some truth.

LARA CROFT

Hi, I'm Angelina. I don't want to start this blog by saying: "Call me Angelina"—that's already so old-fashioned. Besides, I haven't read *Moby Dick*. Actually, I've read very little outside the internet. Today David visited me in the hospital, then left right away. I had been waiting so long for his call that when it finally happened, at the most inopportune moment, while I was talking to the doctor, I felt nothing but annoyed. He brought me an orchid and the nurse placed it in a glass of water on the bedside table. I was afraid that David smelled the same as I did, a stench that was sometimes nauseating: of sweat, of sickness, of a closed room. One of my roommates walked around with her IV hanging out, the other sat in her armchair and looked at David with indifference, as if he were an object.

I'd smelled that same smell before, in the Valdeluz nursing home. There's something old about hospitals, even when they're new and shiny, maybe it's that short stride of the sick, that expression of resignation and exhaustion, like the one my roommate has. But you will never be old, Angelina, you will always smell of perfume, like the one that envelops you when you enter a store in Salamanca or those luxury-brand corners in five-star hotels. It's a special scent, like the countryside, the forest, happiness; a smell of all the good things in life.

David approached my bed.

"You look good, Angelina."

"It's the serum—moisturizes my skin."

He sat down next to me. He'd recently changed jobs, was now selling hearing aids and immersed in the world of marketing. It was very important to delve into all the possibilities of new neuroscience applications that most people were unaware of.

He went on talking for a while, about the odds of getting rich in the emerging hearing-aid market, there were a lot more deaf people than we thought. Then he told me some other news: he had won a Spanish omelet contest. In his spare time he liked to cook and was planning to go on the show *MasterChef.* All his talking was starting to make me dizzy. I wasn't interested in hearing aids or *MasterChef.* I didn't even find as handsome as I used to; his beauty struck me as bland, like a cold sausage for dinner. To think how much I had suffered for this guy and how little I cared about him now!

I saw that he was looking sideways at his cell phone, probably to check the time. I took the opportunity to tell him:

"My dinner will be here soon."

"I'll leave you alone then."

***

Angelina, I hope you don't mind that I've adopted your name. Let me explain everything from the beginning—you still have no idea who I am, even though I know so much about you. But I still think that a life like mine—that of a woman who has never excelled at anything, who will never see her name in the headlines—can still be interesting, even to a star like you. That's why today I've started to write about my memories here on this blog and, if I may be so bold, I'd like you to read it. Everyone matters to someone at some point, don't you think? I'm sorry if I'm nagging you, but I would so much like for you to know me a little—you've just been so fundamental in my life! That's why I dare to ask for your attention. Please, Angelina, if I have managed to get you to start reading my first post, I ask you not to abandon it. Please read on! Just a few minutes of your time, will you?

Angelina, I've felt for many years that the two of us have something in common—silly of me, I know! I'm well aware that we've never met, that the relationship between us is nothing more than a fantasy. I'll tell you how it all happened: it was the day I read in a magazine that your birthday is the same as mine, the same year and everything. What a coincidence! Two years later my younger sister was born, who died when she was five years old, making me an only child.

Reading that we were twins, Angelina, is what sparked my interest in you. I started to follow you more closely—I knew by heart the movies you starred in, what your favorite food was, your favorite color, what the men you fell in love with were like. I was so happy when you gave Brad Pitt that $15 million heart-shaped island, and every time you gave birth or adopted a new child, and when you won the Oscar for Best Supporting Actress and all those Golden Globes. You don't know how proud I was when I found out you were the highest-paid actress in Hollywood or when you embarked on a new career as a director. I just I admire you so much! But I also love you as if I knew you personally, as if we played together when as children and have been friends ever since. I know that you've played so many roles, have brought so many different characters to life onscreen, but for a moment, put yourself in the shoes of a girl like me—imagine playing someone vulgar, a woman of your age, born in Madrid. Angelina, I want you to know something of my life too, even if it's a thousand light years away from yours. You know, we're both Geminis: theatrical, mutable, gifted, giggly, funny and with a certain duality. At least that's what the stars say. In reality, our lives are so different, especially when I think of how much you've achieved in your life and how unlucky I've been in my own. But don't think I'm complaining. No, Angelina, I've been happy so many times!

If you ever bother to read any of my bog posts, you'll see that I'd had many joyful moments. And, even though I'm not famous like you, I want to preserve some of those memories, to keep them stored in the cloud. Like the wild wave of happiness that pummeled me the day I met David.

It was five years ago. Vanesa, my best friend, asked me to go with her to the birthday party of a girl named Eva, a college class-mate of her sister's who was taking advantage of the fact that her parents were away on a trip. Open bar in her garden in Pozuelo. An expensive urbanization in the northern part of the city that has nothing to do with where I live: in Usera, a suburb of Madrid, although we also have a very nice park called Pradolongo.

"Sounds very posh," I told Vanesa.

Vanesa was insistent that I go with her, so there we went, the two of us, in the little hatchback that Vanessa had just bought in installments. We stopped in front of the security booth where guards were posted. A gate flanked the entrance to the garden. Vanessa buzzed in through a video intercom. Eva opened the door: high heels, fresh blonde highlights, professionally-done

make-up, a shiny red miniskirt and a black top patterned with
with lip prints.

"She gets all her outfit inspo from Chiara Ferragni's blog,"
muttered Vanesa, who also looked stunning in a pistachio-green
Zara pantsuit.

Suddenly, I felt insecure in my black dress, walking clumsily
(the new shoes were already hurting) next to Vanessa along the
gravel path in the garden. I remembered something I read in
a self-help book (I'm not much of a reader, but I love self-help
books): "If you want to seduce someone, psych yourself up to go
in for the kill: lift your head a little and think, 'I'm fascinating.'"
The seventeen euros I'd paid for this advice was worth it; repeat-
ing it to myself, I was already starting to feel better.

The smell of jasmine and warm summer fruits heat mixed
with my Rose Arabia perfume. Loudspeakers hidden among the
trees were blasting *Motomami*. Rosalía's voice pierced the air:
"Wearing an F for Fendi / dancing to 'Candy' by Plan B / That's
how you captivated me / the day I met you."

There must have been more than a hundred guests, most of
them girls. They were all scattered between the porch and the
grassy, uniformed cater-waiters swarming among with trays of
drinks. I didn't know anyone. I grabbed a glass of champagne
to calm my nerves. A tall guy approached us, and Vanessa
introduced him to me. He was a perfect ten, but when he kissed
me lightly on the cheek to greet me, I understood that he had
something more than beauty. When I think of the night I met
David, I remember our first encounter as if I were drunk—that
surge of heat in my face, mixed with that shyness that always gets
in the way of these kinds of important moments, that no self-help
trick has ever quelled.

"Do you know you're beautiful?" he said, looking at me as if
he really meant it. "I'd like to dance with you."

It was the first time someone has ever said something like that to me, Angelina. I know it's normal for you to be an object of admiration, but holding hand his hand on the way to the dancefloor I felt like I was walking toward heaven.

"I can't stop looking at you," he said.

I laughed.

"Is that the line you always use when you meet a girl?"

"Only when I like her like I like you. Maybe one in every ten."

"That seems more realistic to me."

"So what do you do for a living?" he asked.

"Guess."

"Model?"

"No."

"Actress?"

"Cold, very cold."

"Singer?"

"Ice-cold."

"I give up."

"I am a nursing assistant in an old folks' home.

"Those are some very lucky old folks!"

I didn't tell him that my boss didn't think so—he didn't even want to renew my crappy contract.

"And what do you do?" I asked him.

"I'm a video game producer."

His job sure sounded much better than mine. I was sure he'd live in Pozuelo or Majadahonda or Las Rozas, like Eva did. But forgive me, Angelina, I have to stop writing—I can hear the rickety noises that announce the arrival of an assistant with the food cart. Goodbye, my dear. Forgive me for calling you like this. See you very soon.

Chapter 2
Effects of Customary Law; Inheritance

The past is like a broken mirror. As you put
it back together, you cut yourself and your
image keeps changing and you change too.

MAX PAYNE 2

It's nine o'clock in the morning on Monday, September 14. My fingers caress the letters on the keyboard of my tablet. I dread the moment when I'm too tired to type. You know how chemo is. But I don't know, Angelina, maybe it's from talking to you, I suddenly feel better, like I'm getting my hopes up again. My mother no longer scolds me like she used to, as if I were still a ten-year-old girl instead of a woman over 40, no longer tells me that I'm wasting my life online, dedicated myself to the lives of people I don't even know. Now she leaves me alone and is sometimes even affectionate with me. Because I spend so much of my time sitting still, I notice things I never noticed before: a fly, a bird, the leaves on a tree in front of my window. One day a salamander came into my room. They say salamanders bring good luck. The attendant shrieked when she saw it and the poor little guy hid under the bed until she left, slamming the door behind her. Then I saw him climbing up the wall, his four little legs clinging to the ceiling.

***

David used to quote lines from his favorite video game characters. One I remember: "The course of time is cruel, different for everyone, and no one can ever change it, but the one thing that does not change with time is the memory of your youth ". Back when I was Mari Pili, my family—an ordinary, lower-middle class family—was the most important thing to me. My grandmother worked as maid until she retired; it's been fifteen years since she died. My mother is a beautician—or an esthetician, as she likes to say. For a while she worked as a masseuse in a nearby gym until she bought a massage table to see private clients, almost all women, for whom she sometimes also does their hair and nails. I've often thought that maybe she was disappointed to have a daughter like me. I think that if you were to ask a group of people what I look like to them, most of them would say that I'm nothing special.

My late sister, however, was very pretty, with a special charm and a permanent smile. In the only photo I have of the two of us, she looks like a little angel, clinging to her Fancy Nancy. You know, Angelina? My face and my body aren't that bad if you look at them separately, but as a whole they lack harmony. On top of that, I have a tendency to put on weight. I have an undeniably vulgar physique. As you'll see from the pictures on my blog, I don't think even the best stylist in Hollywood could do much to improve my appearance. I dress like a housewife who assembles her wardrobe by rummaging through the sales rack at TJ Maxx.

My father works as a security guard. He's proud of his job. I don't think it takes any special qualities to stand by the door of a place that sells food until two in the morning, which is where his bosses have assigned him lately; but he feels like one of Napoleon's marshals, gearing up for a great battle. You have to fool yourself a little to live reasonably contentedly. And that's not what some video game character says—it's what I say. I'm not entirely stupid. Sometimes I think for myself.

***

My mom and dad separated more than ten years ago now. I'd be lying if I said that their separation affected me. I've followed the breakups of so many artists and actors and other celebrities whose lives I follow, that one more separation—even if it was my parents'—couldn't surprise me. Besides, if a couple can't stand each other, the best thing to do is to go their separate ways. Life is too short to suffer more than you have to—I should know, with how bad everything's been for me lately! And all the awful things I've had done to me at the hospital, I'm finally starting to feel better. But back to my parents—neither of them have any money or social skills, though my mother handles herself well with her clients. They're not bad people—I can't complain.

I haven't had much in the way of an education. At the all-girls Catholic school where my parent sent me, I was an below-average student, although I ended up passing the sophomore year after retaking a few classes. Then I found a job nannying on weekends. The children I nannied used to make a big fuss when I was alone with them. I still remember their moods, how they cried when they wanted something. I'm sorry to say that I didn't get attached to any of the little brats. I know you're a great mother to your six children, both biological and adopted, but I was relieved when at the end of each weekend I gave them back to their parents, who were often just as unbearable as their own children.

After my hysterectomy, the doctor told me that my only chance to have children would be through surrogacy, but the news didn't affect me too much. Rather, I was happy to think that I would never have children and, consequently, I would never live in fear that I'd lose them to a terrible accident, like we lost Lara.

***

Before I got sick, my last job was in a nursing home. You see, Angelina, after my time as a nanny, I was a home health aide until Toñi, the social worker who provided me with patients, offered me a position at the Valdeluz Residence. I did well taking care of the elderly. If you manage not to be disgusted by all the disgusting things you have to do, the rest is easy. It was much better than taking care of children, plus having to deal with their unbearable parents. The relatives of old people are usually grateful to those who take care of them properly, and they're not afraid of their loved one's imminent death—unlike the mothers I nannied for who, before leaving for dinner or a weekend trip, would describe in gruesome detail of all the possible accidents that could befall their children that it was my job to avoid.

My life changed forever working at the old people's home. It was there that I met Don Ramiro Téllez de Velarde. Don Ramiro was an ornithologist and naturalist. He had been living in Valdeluz for five years, where he was considered one of its most distinguished residents. He was one of the few people who wanted to help me. If nothing else, I'll always be grateful to him for that. Thanks to his kindness, I managed to improve my personal finances a little and to be disliked even more by some of my coworkers. Especially two of them: Tania, a fat girl with monstrous pimples, and Leila, an uptight fake blonde. Both of them were sharp-tongued, always eager to criticize me or make some nasty comment. I was a regular target of their gossip and envy. But I don't want to go on telling you about these sad excuses for human beings who had it in for me. At the time, all I wanted was to have a good time every now and again, to enjoy life a little—without hurting anyone, Angelina! Perhaps I'm not as caring as you, but I still have ethics.

Today marks two years since I stopped working in Valdeluz. Being a caregiver is definitely not my calling. With some exceptions, like Don Ramiro, the residents were often demanding and complained about me to my supervisor: that I had forgotten to give them their pill, that I didn't pay enough attention to their calls or that I stayed too long in the bathroom. That last one was true because I used to use the mirror above their sink to put on my makeup if I had a date with David, or just to brush my teeth or touch up my hair or put lotion on my hands, which were dry and cracked from so much disinfecting. I don't know why I tell you all these things, Angelina, but I remember what you said in an interview: that very few people are lucky enough to work in what they love. You are privileged in that, as in so many other things.

***

Since I stopped working as a caregiver, I have been able to devote myself to what I am really passionate about, my virtual world, and that's what I want to go back to when I'm cured. Speaking of which, today I got some good news that I want to share with you: the doctor told me that I can go home early next week because my fever broke and my nausea is gone. And he doesn't see any problem with me getting a breast augmentation, but I'll have to wait a year for the wounds to be completely healed. I'm very happy to know that you've also had reconstructive surgery, and that everything went well.

Goodbye, my sunshine. Keep in touch.

Chapter 3
Survival of the Fittest

Love without madness is mere routine.

Up (Walt Disney)

In my younger years, Angelina, I felt like one of those chicks that hatch from the egg kicking, blinded by sunlight. Everything was new and everything hurt. It's how I felt the day I met David, when I learned he really liked me, when I was with him for the first time and the next day he sent me flowers. I remember that after I put them in water I ran excitedly to the phone to call Vanesa. But Angelina, along with some moments of exaltation, I went through others of unbearable pain, moments when life seemed like a cruel and sadistic stepmother, frolicking in the face of my sorrows.

From a very young age, my mother criticized my dreams. I think that deep down she compared me to Lara and imagined what her beautiful daughter, whom she'd named after the protagonist of *Doctor Zhivago*, would have been like at my age. So much so that I sometimes wondered if she would have preferred it if I had been the dead sister and her beautiful Lara the survivor. Mom always insisted on bringing me back to reality, that of our Usera neighborhood, a suburb known for its Chinatown full of trinkets and its youth unemployment rate of 40%. Come on, Mom, why were you so obsessed with trapping me in such a mundane and narrow world?

I look back on myself at 17, 18, 20, 23. It's not until I was 29 that I transformed from Mari Pili into Angelina. A turning point in my life. I rewind back to the night of the party where I met David, how I fell for him so desperately. He looked at me like so many men must look at you, as if I were the only woman in the world, as if he wanted me more than he'd ever wanted anyone else. That night we just danced and talked and drank. Until then I had never had much success with men; the disappointments were piling. But when I met David, I actually believed that we would be together forever. And it seemed we would be, at least at first.

***

My first weekend with David was spent in a house that Vanesa's cousin had lent us in a town in the province of Toledo. Now I realize, Angelina, that I haven't told you about Vanesa. Have you ever noticed those vacation ads with the palm trees and the exotic beach? There's always a girl in a bikini who has just emerged from the sea. Vanesa is like the girls in those ads: brunette, exuberant, smiling, with perfect tits and drops of sea-water sliding down her toasted skin—even in November, up to our necks in our raincoats. Add in some sympathy, some spice, and the look of a woman who always gets what she wants. Armed with all this, it was no wonder that she was a hit everywhere we went: bars, clubs, even on a stroll through the Literary Quarter. The two of us always together: a beautiful panther next to a chubby hyena, ready to pounce. Mario, the photographer, was her latest catch. While many of our friends were getting married or moving in together, Vanesa and I continued with the same life we'd been living since we were teenagers. I even moved back in with my mom; my roommates kicked me out after I couldn't pay my share of the rent for three whole months. Later, Vanessa found a job as a telephone operator in a call center and I took my crappy gig at the Valdeluz Geriatric Residence.

***

The only problem with living with Mom is that around the same time I met David, mom got a boyfriend. Cesar was in the process of separating. He spent every other weekend with his children. On the weekends he had off, he would come on Friday to sleep over. I'd to go have dinner with Dad; we'd eat whatever junk he'd picked up from the takeout place by his house, which was three subway stops from ours. He loved to go there on the nights I had dinner with him, to choose from pizza, salads, or sandwiches, and for dessert, froyo with colorful sprinkles. It was as if Mom and Dad and I had already forgotten about Lara. When I really think about it, our life was nothing special—we were like most families in Usera. But when David stormed into my life, something tipped our precarious family balance. Instead of being happy for me, Mom would nag me for days on end: I didn't help her enough with chores, I treated the house like a hotel, since I had started going out with David she never saw me anymore.

When I arrived home one Friday, after my usual dinner with Dad, Mom and Cesar had clearly just finished having sex and were eating their dinner—leftovers from the previous day—at the kitchen table. Mom was looking at him, rejuvenated, wearing a beatific expression as she cut into a Spanish omelette. César also looked to be in postcoital bliss. It grossed me out a little, seeing them both there drinking their wine and eating their omelette so contentedly, an odd couple, his big belly, her too-tight dress and cheap Chinatown earrings, having had her biweekly orgasm. I decided to take advantage of the moment.

"I wanted to ask you for a bit of money, Mom," I said.

"Again?"

"I can give you some, if you want," César chimed in, with an air of cockiness.

"No, absolutely not!" Mom interjected. "How much do you need?"

"Whatever you can spare."

Mom stormed out of the kitchen and came back with a hundred-euro bill and gave it to me.

"Take it. This is all I can give you until next month—I hope it's enough. Now, see you later!"

She wasn't about to have her sex marathon interrupted. I thanked her and called David.

"Saturday, I'm taking you out," I told him. "The Royal Cantonese—it's one of the best Chinese restaurants in Madrid and it's in my neighborhood. Vanesa had her birthday there last year."

I wasn't going to be cowed by the class difference that separated David and I. According to the new self-help book I was reading, to secure a relationship with the man you love you had to be assertive, positive, confident. We ordered steamed prawns, Cantonese duck, dim sum, and had a couple of Chinese beers each.

"You like this place?"

"It's not bad."

For dessert, we split waffles with chocolate.

As David extended his arm toward the waffles, I noticed that it looked clean, strong, solid. A welcoming arm; I couldn't help but touch it with my hand.

"You don't have any tattoos?"

"I don't need any."

"Angelina Jolie has eight."

"What's that got to do with anything? Besides, I don't care what tattoos you have. I wouldn't like them anyway."

"But you'll like mine. I only have two very discreet ones. Should I get another one with your initials? That way I'll always remember you."

He smiled slightly and I thought that where he lived in Las Rozas people must not like tattoos like they do here in Usera.

He kissed me, grabbed my outstretched hand, and brushed his mouth along the vein that ran from my wrist to the hollow formed by the elbow joint.

"Vanesa invited us to her cousin's house for the weekend" I told him.

Chapter 4
The Acquisition of Beauty

Only in the light does a flower bloom
with beauty. A flower stained with
darkness is destined to wither.

Endrance, hack//g.u.

The next day I had the afternoon free at the nursing home and decided to spend it shopping. I took a bus that passed through downtown Madrid. I walked down Serrano Street, put my hand in the pocket of my pants, and felt the touch of my credit card, fresh and throbbing like a happy sardine. I was fed up with Chinatown shops and even Zara—I had never shopped in a truly expensive store.

The first establishment I stopped in was Roberto Verino, one of my favorite designers.

"Do you have my size?" I asked, pointing to a skirt as the clerk approached me.

"Of course," he replied. "Roberto Verino doesn't just design for young women."

For the first time, at 45, I felt old. What was she implying? That I was past my prime? Was it because I looked like I was wearing TJ Maxx? How old could I be? I fled the store and headed nexdoor to Michael Kors. The store's walls displayed photos of Jacqueline Kennedy and Caroline de Monaco wearing Michael Kors designs. I finally felt like a real shopper, floating in that expensive-store aroma, a faint blend of sandalwood, musk, patchouli, frankincense. Oh, God, the pleasure! A kind clerk left me to my own devices in the fitting room. Maybe it was the intermittent fasting I'd started doing yesterday, or maybe just flattering lighting, but I actually felt attractive. I tried on a little black dress. It was a little tight, but as soon as my diet took effect it would fit perfectly, and the black suited me well. I felt myself getting turned on. I pulled down the silver zipper on the front of the dress to reveal my tits. Reflected in the fitting room mirror—a trick mirror, perhaps, because I looked so good—they swayed a little. Round, firm, soft; one of my strong points. I lifted them up a little with my hand and then kept unzipping the dress. I masturbated right there in front of the magic mirror with my skirt pulled up to my knees.

Ten minutes after buying the dress, I headed to Ekseption, a luxury multi-brand store. The clerks didn't bother me as I looked through the racks of clothes, all designed for women like you, Angelina. For a moment I imagined Lara, too, strolling through the store. She had grown so much lot since I'd seen her last, when she was five. She was now a tall, lithe woman, like a reed, with a mane of curly blonde hair and big blue eyes.

One of the salesmen approached me: a handsome, brown-haired young man, dressed all in black. He reminded me of David. I told him I wanted something sporty for my weekend. He brought me a brown leather Prada jacket and a tight turtle-neck sweater from Dolce & Gabbana. The price was exorbitant.

All the prices in the store were. Then he brought over a pair of Pepe Jeans pants.

"This would go well with what you're wearing."

We talked briefly. At first he seemed rather dismissive until something in me made him realize that I was willing to buy. Then suddenly his tone changed, his voice became huskier and he stared at me and smiled. I was turned on yet again. I thought of him as the fitting room door closed behind me, my arms overflowing with clothes. The pants fit me like a second skin. They say that before you die, you watch your life play back like a movie; in that moment I saw the movie of what my future would be like in these clothes. David and I were drinking and chatting with friends at the ranch where we both lived. Out the window we could see a landscape of mountains, reddened by the twilight sun. He was wearing a brown leather jacket and I was wearing the these Pepe Jeans pants.

At the end of the afternoon, I still had time to go into Kenzo. Inside, a bag immediately seduced me—only a Japanese-American man could design something like it. I slung it over my shoulder and looked in the mirror. The bag made me feel different: modern, young, fun, interesting, striking. All qualities represented by this leather-and-fabric object that I had torn off the arm of a mannequin dressed. When the clerk told me the bag's price, I was perplexed—had it been decorated by Picasso himself? But I couldn't give up this new Angelina I had just met with an extravagant bag slung over her shoulder. I'll buy it," I said, and went through the checkout. I imagined being rung up and met with "I'm sorry, but your card has been declined." A firm hand would snatch from me that singular bag with its perfect balance of beauty and excess, that bag that, brushing against my waistline, would bring out the real me, the Angelina Fernández that I was inside. David's girlfriend, the fashionista, the seductress, the beauty until then hidden among the old people living in the Valdeluz Residence. To my astonishment, the card was accepted and the scanner emitted a noise, like a last gasp of my VISA before handing over everything I'd saved from seven years of taking care of those awful people.

Chapter 5
How I Evolved to Become an Angelina

There is so much to learn and you know so little.

ANSEM (KINGDOM HEARTS)

Angelina, I want to tell you about my childhood. My parents named me Pilar after my grandmother. When I was little they called me Mari Pili, but when you came into my life I decided to change my name and adopt yours. I believe that one should choose one's own features, height, and complexion, just as we decide who we marry or who we befriend. One day I decided to look like you. First, in name. Names are important; they're the door through which things, ideas, people enter. I admired you so much that I wanted your name and mine to sound the same, so at the age of 29, I stopped being Maria del Pilar Fernández and became Angelina Fernández. The decade that followed was a blur! I had several relationships, but none worth mentioning. Sometimes it seemed like there was something in me that pushed me toward loneliness.

With your name, Angelina, I enjoyed the best years of my youth. Don't think that everything has been bad! No! I've had wonderful moments that I want to share! That's why I've started writing this blog, trying to communicate with you, although I know you'll never answer. I confess that this blog has almost no followers. Since I started writing weekly *posts*, a few readers have popped by for a peek at my thoughts, my memories, my stories from my forty-five years on this earth. If you've been reading this far, you already know that I've never had the ambition nor the self-confidence necessary to make something of myself in life. But I've always liked to learn. And recently, the internet has made possible a kind of learning some might call intellectual. But back to David.

Vanessa's cousin's town was 50 kilometers down the road from Toledo. David and I drove there in his car. I was wearing my new Pepe Jeans and carrying my new designer handbag. I am admittedly a bit superstitious; I thought that new clothes would bring me luck. I didn't want to think, however, about how my walk along the Golden Mile in Salamanca had depleted my savings. In the car David queued up playlist.

"Do you like classical music?" he asked me.

"Yes." I said to say something.

"It's Mozart," he said.

I closed my eyes and let myself be transported by the sounds that enveloped me. It was the first time someone had ever told me about this Mozart person. His name rang a bell, but I'd never heard any of his records.

"I love it," I said.

It was true. I had never heard anything like it, so sad and joyful at the same time, and if I had to choose a single, perfect scene to rescue from my vulgar life, I would go back to that summer morning, in the seat of David's dusty Toyota SUV, listening to Mozart, next to him, for the first time.

The GPS took us to a development of five-story houses on the outskirts of town. Vanesa was waiting for us at one of the entrances with her boyfriend of the moment, a photographer for an Italian magazine. She opened the door of the house with the key that Marcos, her cousin who was on vacation in Alicante, had left her. When we entered, I no longer regretted having spent in one afternoon almost everything I had saved. When David and I lived together, we would live in a single-family house, probably in the country, or at least in a good housing development, I decided. I don't know why I was sure that we would end up rich and would be able to buy a house somewhere special that we both liked.

Vanesa and the photographer went ahead to claim the best room. David and I settled in the only room that was available, a two-by-two-meter crawl space. From the window of the mini bedroom we could see the countryside, spoiled by industrial buildings. The best thing was the bed, a Japanese futon with its rice straw tatami, which occupied three-quarters of the room, where we messed around for a while before going to the kitchen.

Vanesa had brought ready for the four of us. We all sat down at the kitchen table and she told us about her job at the call center and her more than 50,000 followers on Instagram. She was thinking of becoming a full-time influencer, promoting fashion brands. After all our fun on the navy-blue futon, I felt the part of my body in most intimate contact with my jeans burning, and all I could think about was David. His legs, muscled by the elliptical he used at the gym where he went after work, touched my thighs under the table. And silly me, instead of living in the moment, I started thinking that maybe I wasn't attractive enough for him and that maybe he didn't like me enough to stay. After dinner we went for a walk around town. By the time David and I returned to our love nest, it was already three in the morning. I took off my New Balance sneakers and Pepe Jeans and was left in just my mid-thigh length black stockings and leather jacket.

"You look beautiful," he said.

He was panting. In the distance I could hear the engine of the cars driving along the road. Through the window, I saw the glow of the streetlamps. When he lunged at me, our bodies reflected like shadow puppets in the windows.

The next day, David suggested we have a picnic in the countryside with the food Vanesa had brought and the ham and cheese I'd bought with my credit card before stashing in David's drawer where it would never again see the light of day. For a moment I thought about what my mother would say if she found out that I'd spent almost all my savings in an afternoon of shopping.

Vanesa spread out a blanket, put a checkered tablecloth on top and brought out the food and the plastic plates and glasses with the help of her new beau. The industrial buildings were far away; from here we could see only oaks trees. I breathed the air full of wild aromas. I hardly knew the countryside. When I was a child, on Sundays the whole family would go to the mall. But there was one day... A landscape opened up in the fog of my memory. Lara and I walking hand in hand with Mom and Dad.

Mom had spread a tablecloth on the grass and the four of us sat down near the water. We could hear the hoarse murmur of a river. I sat next to Dad and Mom took Lara by the hand and began to feed her pieces of a Spanish omelette from a pan. Where would that have been? The trees were beautiful. I had almost forgotten about that excursion. Otherwise, my life has been totally urban—I've only known the countryside from my favorite TV shows. But that day, near the village where Vanesa's cousin had his house, in that no man's land on top of a hill, it seemed to me that I smelled spring for the first time.

David fixed his green eyes on my cleavage, enhanced by my new top from La Perla. I had done some more shopping prior to the excursion, though I won't bore you with the details, Angelina, but one of the things I bought was this lycra top, which I was wearing now, and it looked great on me, or so I thought at the time. I was also staring at his jeans, which looked like they were about to pop. I'd never been so horny, and neither had he. His face was even more telling than the size of his penis.

"Let's go."

"We have to eat. There's no time," I said, pursing my mouth and giving a look somewhere between prissy and mischievous.

"We'll be right back."

David was dragging me by the arm. He looked possessed, like a madman, pulling me along behind him. We walked toward an old, abandoned shed. The wooden door gave way at the first kick. Then he pushed me against the wall, grabbed me by the head, and gripped me wildly as I stripped naked, our shared sense of urgency erupting in a barrage of moans. As he ran his tongue and hands all over me, my clothes fell to the floor. I was left with only my stockings up to mid-thigh, sweltering in the heat of my own passion. I closed my eyes as David kissed me in the darkness of the shed.

When we returned, Vanessa and the photographer greeted us impatiently.

"Come on, you guys took forever—we were starving!"

Vanessa smiled her shampoo-commercial smile.

"Didn't enough last night?"

The photographer put his arm around her shoulder.

"Questo è l'amore, cara."

We started to eat and Mario said that our lunch reminded him of a painting by Manet called—I don't know how to pronounce it in French, Angelina, but it translates to *The Luncheon on the Grass*. Mario and David started to talk about art, and they seemed to get along very well; none of Vanessa's and my friends ever talked about things like that. Vanesa started to tell me about the new website she'd launched all about the latest trends and luxury brands and, of course, of her nearly 51,000 followers on Instagram. She also hadn't heard of Manet or *Lunch on the Grass* and Mario explained that it was like a super-luxury brand within the world of Impressionist painting. At dessert we took a lot of photos on our phones. I loved watching David eat and hand out chorizo slices and pour wine. Joy spilled out onto the grass with every laugh and every comment, as if we were at one of Manet's luncheons, and I thought I had never loved anyone as much as I loved David and would never love anyone like we loved each other. Then Vanessa broke the spell a little bit when she asked David about the girls he was casting for commercials, a side job he did when he wasn't working at the video game production company, and I imagined all those gorgeous women that my boyfriend saw every day, my potential competitors. But in spite of everything, that day I saw myself exactly as I wanted to be, as if the golden light, filtered by the oak tree branches that embellished my features in the photos that Vanesa took of us, had brought out the Angelina that I felt inside me. That's why I want to remember that excursion in my blog post today, to preserve that day, to rescue it from oblivion. I know it's nothing special, Angelina, but for me it was very important. I wanted to share it with you too.

Chapter 6
Secondary Sexual Characteristics

What is a man but the sum of his memories!

ASSASSIN'S CREED

That first weekend David and I spent together was followed by others. David invited me on short trips around Spain and we even went abroad: a long weekend in Paris and two weeks in Santorini.

In the Valdeluz Residence, in spite of everything, the work was less stressful than nannying: these grandparents were better behaved than the sadistic little snots who threw tantrums at the drop of a hat. You can end up cajoling old people with some kind words, by speaking slowly and sweetly; children, not so much. The old people— I tell you, Angelina! They used to follow my orders, take the medicines without complaint. I would leave them wrapped in a blanket in their wheelchairs to watch TV for a little while. Some of them tugged their IVs or looked down at their wadded-up slippers with resignation; others spent the whole day half-asleep with their mouths ajar like a piggy bank.

Don Ramiro Téllez de Velarde, my favorite, was a dry, wiry, and cultured gentleman—a nature-lover and amateur ornithologist. He was very well-educated, who always asked me for things politely and never forgot to thank me. With him I did some extra work as an escort to supplement my income.

On some of my days off I used to take Don Ramiro for a walk to get some fresh air. He wait for me around ten o'clock in the morning and when I went to pick him up he was already dressed for his stroll. Afterwards we would go shopping and have lunch at a really good restaurant, which made it difficult to keep up my diets. I made up for it by getting a personal trainer, to which Don Ramiro's generosity contributed. Thanks to me, he was no longer alone. Ever since he came to Valdeluz, he hadn't had any visitors, even though his two nephews, who lived in Brussels, visited Madrid every Christmas.

To celebrate the holidays, Don Ramiro and I went shopping in Salamanca. It was dusk, the lights were shining, and the cafés and restaurants and art galleries breathed a mist of warm lust. I saw my images reflected in the storefront windows, like that time David and I had our shadow-puppet show. The old man was excited to buy me some Bulgari earrings and a Dolce & Gabbana skirt. But what I liked most about Don Ramiro was his liberality, his attentions were not reserved to myself and the next day he invited my boyfriend and me to dinner.

We went to Cappuccino, a trendy café on a covered terrace, heated by stoves with red-hot coals that reminded me of the round chestnut kettles where my mother used to buy Lara and me a warm nuts on winter Sundays. As we were having our first course, a spectacularly sexy and slutty-looking woman walked in; worse, she approached our table and greeted David warmly. He got up to kiss and hug her and reciprocate her caresses, then introduced us to Carlota, that was this woman's name. He introduced

Don Ramiro with his full name, Ramiro Téllez de Velarde, and then to me by my name, without adding "my girlfriend" or "my partner" or anything else that would make Carlota think that we were in a relationship. He knew exactly what he was doing.

"Carlota is a freelance video game programmer. She collaborates with our production company from time to time," said David. "Angelina," he added, looking at me and then at Carlota, "works in a nursing home."

Being a videogame programmer sounded much better than working in a nursing home. I remembered my self-help books and tried to assert myself.

"I love my job," I said. "I've always loved taking care of others, ever since I was a little girl."

Don Ramiro smiled as if to encourage me.

"Do you want to have a drink with us?" David asked Carlota.

It felt like I'd been punched in the stomach, but I hid it as best I could.

Don Ramiro, polite as ever, stood up while Carlota sat between David and him, facing me. She had the stove next to her and took off her jacket. Her navy-blue top clung to a pair of fake tits and arms reshaped with weights and aerobics. Up close, her face was just average, except for her hazel eyes, big and sweet as if they'd been dipped in honey.

Carlota ordered a *gin and tonic*, as did I. Don Ramiro ordered a Coca-Cola and David a *whiskey*. Then David told the waiter to bring us shrimp rolls and some other appetizers, his tone strangely domineering.

When the appetizers came and then disappeared without my having taken a bite, David, who seemed to be calling the shots that night, said to everyone, "Come on, why don't you order another drink? Or something else to eat. Here, have some ham skewers."

The three of us politely refused and David discreetly got up from the table. Later, when Don Ramiro asked for the bill, the waiter said, looking at David, that it was already paid for.

"But how!" Don Ramiro protested. "*I* invited *you!*"

"Next time," said David.

Carlota left first—she had to work the next morning. Maybe she would meet David again in his office, where she used to go to present some of the video games she had programmed. Maybe they'd talk about their meeting the day before and Carlota would mention to me, in passing, the way you talk about someone who hasn't caught your attention.

"You two seem very friendly," I said to David when Carlota finally left.

"She's a very nice girl," he replied.

I went to the bathroom and called Vanesa, crying. After talking to her for a while I felt better. Vanesa is very smart—she has so many Instagram followers for a reason—and she got me to calm down enough to go back to the table.

"Sorry," I said. "I just ran into a friend I haven't seen in a while."

Don Ramiro gave me a knowing look. I went with him back to the residence. In the hall of Valdeluz was an artificial pine tree decorated with cardboard boxes underneath and a giant star on top. Leila was in the hallway and when we arrived. She looked at her watch: I was an hour late for my night shift. I didn't doubt for a moment that she would see to it that our manager heard about my tardiness. I went with Don Ramiro into his room. Immediately Tania appeared, sniffing like a bloodhound.

"It's very late for Don Ramiro," she said dryly, looking only at me as if the old man were an inanimate object. "At ten o'clock you should have given him his medication and taken his blood pressure."

"A day is a day," said Don Ramiro to the shrew with his characteristic kindness. But she still wouldn't leave.

Since I was growing so fond of him, I always tried to provide Don Ramiro with some kind of distraction. That night he had brought him a magazine with pictures of his favorite girls, just some light porn, none of that filthy stuff that assaults the sensibilities. Tania gave the magazine a sidelong glance. She moved a little closer to the table, her fierce eyes narrowing on the cover.

I was sure that as soon as I left she was going to pick it up and leaf through it. I gave her a look full of contempt. Finally, she left with a characteristic gesture of disgust and closed the door behind her. I put a diaper on under Don Ramiro's pajamas and gave him his dose of half a sleeping pill. Then I went to attend to Mariuca, another resident, who was in her nineties and had removed her cannula. I paged the on-call nurse to put it in.

When I finished my work it was eight o'clock in the morning and I was so exhausted that I didn't even have the strength to think about David. Angelina, my dear, I hope I'm not boring you. I'll tell you more later.

Chapter 7
The Struggle for Existence

It is amazing what a person can forget, but it
is even more amazing what they can hide.

TIFA LOCKHART

Unfortunately, our walks, which were so good for Don Ramiro, had to be cut short when he developed a degenerative disease. His legs began to fail and, as he did not like to go out in a wheelchair, he had no choice but to stay at the residence all the time, watched over by those vermine, Tania and Leila. I would arrive half an hour before my shift and go into his room. He was beginning to lose his voice and was already very hard to understand. We established a system of hand signs to communicate. Sometimes I was exasperated by how difficult it was for him to express the simplest things. His ability to understand, however, remained intact.

"You know what, Don Ramiro?" I said to him one day. "I hardly see my boyfriend David these days. I don't think he loves me anymore."

He gave me a look in which I thought I sensed a hint of compassion.

"I'd like to see you with less clothes on," he suggested in his new language.

I forgot to tell you, Angelina, that Don Ramiro was something of a voyeur, though quite harmless otherwise. He was generally content to settle for glimpses of some female flesh to satisfy his tired, senile libidino, or to just look at erotic magazines and videos. Now that he could no longer walk around like he used to and was confined to the nursing home all day, he was bored out of his mind. I went into his bathroom to undress and came out naked, perched on my high heels like a stilt walker. He was starting to breathe heavily—he sounded like he was going to have a heart attack—when I heard footsteps in the heallway, approaching the door. I ran back into his bathroom and quickly changed into my uniform. When I came out, Tania was with him. She looked curiously at my tousled hair and the belt of my half-tied robe.

"Don't you have other patients to attend to?" she said.

Tania was the type of woman who always had greasy hair. She must have had some sort of untreated seborrhea. Beneath her black, clumpy locks, her face was pockmarked by acne. Now, in the florescent light, I could see all of her pimples. I remembered that one day when I saw her changing she had some kind of nasty erysipelas on her back. I never understood why our supervisor didn't at least force her to pull back her hair.

"Don Ramiro has to sleep. It is very late."

"That's for him to decide," I replied.

"You have other residents to attend to," she said angrily. "Don't linger too long in here." Then she left.

I laid Don Ramiro down for the night and left—I couldn't risk staying in his room any longer. I spent the night on call dozing off in a chair and answering residents' calls every time the light came on. I looked at my texts, there was one from David:

next weekend he couldn't stay in Madrid with me. He had a job—he didn't specify which one. Another message from Mom with her perennial warnings, and from Vanesa, who wanted to know what was up. I didn't feel like telling her anything about the sad epilogue of my relationship with David. I replied that I had a lot of work to do at the residence and asked her about her life and her luxury-lifestyle website and the companies that paid her to promote their products.

At eight o'clock in the morning I finished my night shift. I went down to the cafeteria for breakfast. In spite of everything, I was hungry. I had a coffee, juice, toast, and three croissants. At nine o'clock, before going home, I decided to say goodbye to Don Ramiro. When I came into his room, Leila was helping him get dressed. When she was done, she left him sitting in his ergonomic chair and went to attend to other residents. I went into his bathroom and took off my uniform. Don Ramiro let out a little grunt of approval when he saw me walk out naked in my high heels. I put some cushions under him. Through the window, the morning light metabolized like orange ice cream.

It was nice to think that I could finally do whatever I wanted, freely, with no one else watching but that little old man with his soft little sighs. At last I felt uninhibited. I put on a pair of stockings, which I fastened above the knee with my silicone garters. We looked together at the girls in the magazine I had brought him. He said he liked that kind of magazine—it reminded him of when he used to sneak copies of *Playboy* in his youth—but I didn't dare to bring him any more lest they get confiscated. I sat down next to Don Ramiro, who was smiling. What was wrong with giving the poor man a little happiness in this finallast stage of his life?

The bodies of each of the girls in the magazine were very different: some fleshy, some slim; some with giant breasts, some with narrow hips; and a myriad of possible combinations. Finally a man appeared, a jock, built like an athlete. I imagined him in riding boots and spurs, on the ranch I shared with David in my imagination. In the picture he was straddling a brunette with long, shiny hair and a huge ass in the middle of a forest. From Don Ramiro's room I could smell leaves, grass, and smoke seemed to reach Don Ramiro's room, could hear the shearing of a flock of sheep. Later, that cretin of a psychiatrist would tell me that the ranch was only a fantasy of my subconscious that functioned as an inducing stimulus. Typical for an obsessive neurotic like me.

By the time we tired of looking at the magazine pictures, shreds of digested light were coming through the window—reds, blues, greens that heralded twilight. I was naked from the waist down, except for my stockings and heels, so I put on the black silk shirt Don Ramiro had presented me as the finale of our shopping season. I wanted to make a TikTok to give to him; he had one of those cell phones that's only good for phone calls, but he could watch it on mine. I filmed myself dancing around a bit and even did some of the stuff I'd seen in the late-night movies on Channel 8. In that oment I could relate to you a little bit, Angelina. Don Ramiro would just watch—I wouldn't have let him touch me. I moved around to a reggaeton song. When I played back the video, I muted the music—the last thing I needed was for Leila or Tania to come in and see Don Ramiro and me indulging in our little games! Suddenly, I was in a good mood, perched on a peak of euphoria. In the skin of another girl: successful, smiling, beautiful and fun; as rich as Eva with that impressive chalet in Pozuelo, the one at the party where I met David; as beautiful as Vanesa. I wish I had a job where I wouldn't have to deal with sad things like aging and illness and death all day long. To be a fashion influencer like Vanesa with thousands of followers, paid by luxury brands to promote their products. I made sure the door was locked before releasing what my psychiatrist later diagnosed as "repressed libidinal energy," which erupted at the climax of my dance... Then I got dressed very slowly, putting on my skirt, wool sweater, jacket, and printed scarf around my neck. I combed my hair and put on my bright red lipstick.

I looked at myself again. In my reflection in the bathroom mirror there was still the memory of his my recent nudity. When I came out, already dressed, Don Ramiro waved goodbye.

"Looking very elegant at this early hour," Tania said as she passed me in the hall with a touch of mockery.

***

That night I was supposed to have dinner with Dad. He called me. Instead of having takeout at his house, he invited me to a restaurant. He'd noticed something was up with me. I was glad to see him and free myself for a few hours from my mother's presence at home. Since I had moved back in with her, she treated me as if I were a teenager. I couldn't stand her constant nagging. And now that David had ghosted me, I spent most of my free time on the internet, which got on Mom's nerves.

"Don't you have anything better to do than to be hooked up to the computer all day" she said.

You would think, with how much she criticizes the way that I spend my time, that she falls asleep reading *Don Quixote* every night, with César beside her listening to Beethoven. But Mom likes to think that she has given me a very rigorous education. I still remember the time when my parents lived together. I see them having dinner. There's a tray in front of the TV, Mom is in the kitchen cleaning up while Dad gobbles down the remains of a pizza, nachos with guacamole, tortilla chips with a beer, and all sorts of edible filth. This is how we spent every night, from nine to midnight, watching stupid quiz shows or phony *reality shows*. I know, Mom, that's what home has always meant to you, and that's what you've always wanted for me: a husband eating in front of the TV. That's why you never understood why Dad left to look for happiness elsewhere. I know it was yet another blow after Lara.

I remember, before Dad left, when you would come into the little living room where we watched TV to pick up the tray with the leftovers, and you would suddenly stand there for a while, lost in thought. Then Dad and I would look at each other because we both knew that at that moment you were thinking about my sister. A little angel in heaven, the neighbors said when they came to pay their condolences. And you never forgave Dad for consoling himself so soon with Rita. And me? Did you forgive me? Anyway, you know what? I know you weren't perfect, but you did what you could. I can't pin all my neuroses on you.

***

At the restaurant, Dad ordered his favorite meal: scallops with french fries. Since Rita had left him—taking with her, in the process, a good part of what he had saved over his years of working as a security guard—he had put on weight and looked grim.

"Do you have a problem, Angelina?" he asked me. "If it's about money, you know I don't have much, but I'd like to help you in any way I can."

"No—thank you, though. Money's not the issue."

"It'd be great if they made you staff at the nursing home. You need some security."

Dad was obsessed with job security. I didn't tell him that my supervisors were probably not going to renew my contract.

"Look how many years I've been with the same company!" I said. "I'm going to be 40 years old. Just five more to go before I retire."

I smiled at him.

"You haven't eaten much," he said. "Didn't you like the place?"

"It's great, but I wasn't very hungry."

"You're not on a diet again, are you?" he said as he paid the bill.

"No, Dad."

"I'm glad. I'm going to walk with you home. I don't like you out alone at this hour." We went to leave the restaurant. "You don't think about it anymore, do you?" he asked me out of the blue.

He must have been referring to Lara's accident.

"No," I lied.

"We have to try and live the best we can every day, honey," he said.

I was already familiar with his various words of wisdom; they were all pretty similar and I knew most of them by heart. We walked at a good pace. I had sent a message to David telling him that it had been a long time since we had seen each other. My birthday was coming up and I wanted to invite him again to the Royal Cantonese. I would wait until I got home to read his reply.

Chapter 8
Slavery Instinct

Don't depend on anyone in this world...
Because even your own shadow
leaves you in the dark.

Vergil

When I got home, the apartment looked messier than usual. Dirty dishes were piling up in the kitchen sink. As her relationship with Cesar progressed and Mom devoted more time to couple's activities and grooming herself, the clutter in our apartment had grown. Still, it felt like I was returning to my safe place, far from the exotic lands and name brands of Serrano where money was taken for granted, far from the splendorous scenery that I frequented with Don Ramiro and the glittering landscape that for a short time I traveled with David. Here I was my true self, the Pilar/Angelina that I had never stopped being. I was very tired and lay down on my bed to read my texts. David had not answered me, but I had a message from Vanesa.

Vanesa: How's it going? I haven't heard from you in a while.

Me: Bad with David.

Vanesa: You've been saying that forever. Forget it already.

Me: When you like someone, it takes a long time to forget them.

Vanessa: Then do what *you* feel like doing. If you want to, call him.

ME: I'm afraid he'll think I'm a pain in the ass.

Vanessa: So what if he does! What do you care!

Me: I'm afraid he'll act out again. The sooner he forgets me, the better! But when I do call him, I do it for me. Even if it's all an illusion, even if there's no future for us, just seeing him feels like this injection of happiness and energy that makes up for everything else.

Vanessa: I completely understand!!!!!!!! It's all just a fantasy.

Me: I don't know if I should wait or call him now... but what if he doesn't respond?

Vanessa: You'll live.

Me: I've barely even seen him these past few months. He's just leading me on, leaving breadcrumbs.

Vanessa: When a guy really cares about you, he doesn't act like that.

I turned off my phone. I wasn't lying when I told Dad that I never thought about Lara anymore. I hadn't thought about her for a long time, but suddenly, there in my bed, I felt her close to me. I saw her with the face she might have grown up to have. She smiled at me, and I put my arms around her neck, through her tangle of golden blond hair. She consoled me until I fell asleep and dreamed of David again.

At about three in the morning, I heard Mom and Cesar go into Mom's bedroom.

"Since it's Saturday, I'm going to spend the day with César in Aranjuez," Mom told me the next morning, holding out four 50-euro bills. "I want you to go to the supermarket."

The shopping center on Marcelo Usera Street was crowded. People were walking around, grabbing what they needed and perusing the shelves. They were elbowing one another over canned goods and vegetables and plastic-wrapped fruits as if they were stockpiling supplies in preparation for a siege. I grabbed some donuts, muffins, frozen pizzas—too many carbohydrates—and tossed in a few fruits, a spring salad, and some microwavable veggies.

***

When I returned home from the supermarket, I didn't feel like going out again so I spent the afternoon sitting in front of my computer. I felt better when I was online. I visited a few dating sites—Matching Friends was the one I liked the most. The feeling that someone wants you, even virtually, is very gratifying for a girl like me—awkward, insecure, and newly boyfriend-less. You can't imagine, Angelina, how many people can only express their desires from behind a computer screen. Protected by anonymity, I've learned how to present myself and how to hide at the same time, to be both generous and elusive. I wish you could see them, these guys I agreed to video chat with, moaning, panting, begging me for a date. You don't know how arousing it can be to exhibit yourself like that, exposed but veiled, shielded from the outside by screen, delivering a sweet soliloquy—David taught me that word—to my computer. Yes, David taught me many things, including how bad it feels to get ghosted.

Ah! And my name, Angelina, which I have already adopted forever in your honor, works very well online, people think it's a pseudonym.

***

When I went to visit Don Ramiro in the residence the next morning, a nurse in uniform who was not part of the Valdeluz staff was with him. My colleagues told me that his two nephews and their wives had decided to hire a private health aide to take care of him. His nephews, absent for so long, had suddenly decided to show up, planting themselves at his side at all hours. They immediately let me know that my presence was not necessary. The two men and one of the women, an unhappy Belgian woman who spat when she spoke, took turns to never leave him alone.

One morning I saw Don Ramiro's door ajar. I pushed it slightly and peeked through the crack: the room was dark, both the aide and the family must have left. Don Ramiro was alone, sitting in his ergonomic chair. I went in and greeted him with a kiss him on the cheek. He was finding it increasingly difficult to speak, making guttural noises that had to be interpreted. His health had worsened considerably since the last time I saw him. It would be prudent, I thought, to move him to another specialized residence or to his own home, where he could be under the supervision of a roster of caregivers, but from what I could understand from his hand signals, his vulture nephews had rented his 400-square-meter apartment on Serrano Street and got Valdeluz to agree to his staying there.

"They want to incapacitate me," Don Ramiro had told me in his labored sign language.

He pointed to the bottom drawer of the dresser. I opened it. It was full of papers. I got up to close the door. I trembled at the thought that someone might come in and see me rummaging through his things. Don Ramiro was shaking his head as I pulled out his mementos: letters and old photos, one of which showed him in a restaurant with his ex-wife. They were both smiling.

"Your wife was very beautiful," I said. He had never told me about her.

Apparently, there was not much to explain. She had left him for one of his best friends more than 40 years ago and he had been living alone ever since. He never had children with the woman in the photo.

I took out more papers, one at a time, but Don Ramiro continued to shake his head. There was also a collection of fetish objects: postcards of women in high heels, corsets, and a small black leather whip. Finally, I found what he was looking for: an old pharmacy prescription on yellowing paper topped with the Globo Pharmacy logo, which was a little drawing of a hot air balloon. The prescription, which must have been at least 40 years old, was for batracotoxin.

"I don't think this will help you, Don Ramiro," I told him. "You need a more recent prescription."

I looked up the address of El Globo Pharmacy, which still existed near Arenal Street. Don Ramiro asked me to check the drawer for his leather-bound address book, the kind people kept before you could store your contacts in your phone. Inside it, I found a name: Enrique Gallardo.

"He's a friend of mine whom I trust a lot," he explained to me with his signs and sounds. I was starting to become an expert in his language. "I'm sorry to bother you."

"It's no trouble at all," I replied. "It's the least I can do for you and I'll be happy to do it."

This was partly true—my shopping sprees with Don Ramiro were some of the happiest times of my life, and for that I've always been grateful. Of course, perhaps the old man's fondness for me was influenced by what he used to call our little follies. It also said a lot about his gentleness that he accepted that I didn't touch him, he was too old and that would have been disgusting to me.

When I returned home, Mom was gone. She'd been going out a lot more, like a young woman just starting to discover life. I pulled a scrap of paper from my purse, with the name "Enrique Gallardo" written in block letters and a phone number. I dialed all nine digits. I got the answering machine and left Don Ramiro's name and my phone number, so that the conversation wouldn't be intercepted. I added that Mr. Téllez de Velarde would very much like to speak to Mr. Gallardo. Then I slept until three in the afternoon—my shift had left me exhausted—and ate alone in front of the TV set, thinking about David again. What had I done to make him leave me with no explanation? Then again, deep down I always knew he would.

Chapter 9
The Friendly Species

The greatest affliction is to remember
the happy moments in sadness.

Dante's Inferno

I sent David another text, but when I went to check if he was online, the icon that usually contained his profile picture was empty. I tried Facebook, but still couldn't access his profile. He'd blocked me. I called Vanesa.

"Why do you think he did it?" she asked.

"In the end, I was sending him like 50 messages a day."

"You overwhelmed him."

"You told me not to worry about being a burden!"

"But you shouldn't act crazy either. Forget it—don't ever think about him or call him again," Vanesa concluded.

I had an afternoon shift at the residence. When I arrived, half an hour late, I put on my uniform and went to see Don Ramiro. The supervisor had told me that his aide had taken the day off and that there was also a new assistant, Marta, taking over for our colleague Alba while she was on maternity leave. The new assistant greeted me with joy.

"Thank goodness you're here," she said to me. "I couldn't take any more of this old man. I think the psychiatrist at the nursing home should see him—he says some weird stuff. Do you think I should report him for harassment?"

"No," I said. "He's lost his mind and can barely speak."

"But his hands still work."

Marta had fair skin and hazel eyes, very pretty. I found her very amusing, especially compared to the other assistants, who always looked like they had a stomach ache. David would have called her :a very nice girl."

"He has a safe in his room. He seems to have a lot of money, unlike the rest of the old folks who live on their pensions. Honestly, if a plague came to this residence and everyone died it would take a load off Social Security."

Her vitality was infectious and, for the first time in a long time, I laughed heartily.

"I'm glad you work here," I said. "I'm having a tough time right now, and all my roommates here hate me."

"No way!" Marta quickly said. "They're just jealous."

"Are you from here?"

"Yeah, why?"

"I thought you might be South American, from Venezuela or something. There's something exotic about your face, it reminds me of Angelina Jolie's. Has anyone ever told you that?"

"No, but I'm glad you did."

"I gotta go," I told her. "If they see the two of us chatting instead of working, they'll tear us a new one.

I said goodbye to Don Ramiro, put the old recipe with the master formula in my bag and left the room, lest his nephews arrive, for they took turns to never leave him alone.

The next day Enrique Gallardo called me back and we arranged to meet at the residence at nine o'clock that night, when
Don Ramiro's relatives would no longer be hovering around
his room.

When I saw Enrique walking down the hallway I knew
it was hi: a slim man with white hair and a pleasant smile. He
must have been very handsome when he was young. He was very
well-dressed, although a bit old-fashioned: loafers, polo shirt,
sports jacket. He looked like one of those distinguished foreign-
ers you see at a five-star hotel; I guessed he was about 70 years old.

"Excuse me miss," he said to me, "do you by any chance know
Don Ramiro Téllez de Velarde?"

"Yes, Room 323," I said. "Are you Enrique Gallardo?"

"The very same."

"Don Ramiro asked me to call you because he was very interested in seeing you. We have half an hour before visiting hours
are over."

When we entered his room, Don Ramiro looked very upset.

"What's the matter with him?" Enrique said. "Calm down,
for God's sake!"

I took Don Ramiro's hand, took his pulse.

"Don't worry," I said to him. "I'm on duty again tonight. I'll
keep you company."

"Hello, Ramiro," said Enrique, taking Don Ramiro's hand.
"I'm your old friend. I'm here for whatever you need."

Don Ramiro seemed to calm down and pointed to a drawer
in his bureau. Since he was in a suite, one of the most expensive
rooms in the residence, he had been allowed to bring some of his
furniture with him.

Enrique opened the drawer. It was full of papers. With nimble
hands he went through them quickly; he seemed to know what
he was looking for. He stopped for a moment at a particular doc-

ument, three or four pages with the same letterhead stapled together. He put them in his jacket pocket.

"Leave everything to me," he said to his friend.

Someone knocked on the door. Luckily, it was Marta. I introduced her to Enrique then prepared her for her shift.

"So you'll need to take his temperature and give him his sleeping pills," I explained to her. "Here are the charts where you have to write down all the medicines he's taken and at what time. And this is a chart for you to write down the temperature."

By the time Enrique and I left, Don Ramiro had calmed down and even smiled at us.

"We'll be in touch," Don Ramiro's friend told me as he said goodbye. "I'm very grateful that you called me."

He gave me his business card: "Enrique Gallardo, Madrid Notary." I put it in my purse along with the old pharmacy prescription.

I don't know, Angelina—maybe all these things I'm telling you about my past life don't interest you at all. I don't think a nursing home is the most fascinating place in the world either, but it's what I know, the only real job I've ever had. Forgive me if I'm boring you with these old stories. Until my next entry. Good night, my dear.

Chapter 10
Plumage, Laws
of Its Change

Happy endings are unfinished stories.

MR. AND MRS. SMITH

When I returned to the apartment, Mom was eating dinner alone in the kitchen. When she saw me, she immediately went into conversation mode.

"It's been a long time since I've seen David," she said.

"We broke up."

"Well, I always thought he was shady anyway. Too cool for my taste. You'll find someone better, don't worry."

From time to time, Mom would proselytize positive thinking. She looked at me closely. Had I put on a few pounds in the last few days? I nodded grumpily. I'd been spending less time with my personal trainer and more time shopping. She launched into a rant: she always found time to take care of herself after work and I should do the same.

"Can you just top talking for a second? I'm getting dizzy."

"I'll shut up if you want," he replied, offended. "I was thinking of going out with César, but I didn't want you to be alone. Are you sure you'll be all right?"

"Yes, don't worry. I'm fine, really! Go live your life."

I went to my room and sat for a moment in front of my new computer, the latest Apple laptop, replacing my old HP. I opened it up and ran my fingers across its keyboard. It looked like one of those white pianos you see in Hollywood movies. I browsed through some old chats. I'd recently seen on TV a spacecraft that NASA had sent to Venus: the robot Curiosity was walking around a desolate planet, no sign of life, just a set of grayish craters, free from the anxieties and anguish that grip all of us back on Earth. Curiosity had been programmed to leave a message that could be picked up by some alien. Of course the aliens wouldn't speak our language, so the robot scattered drawings of a man and a woman, representative of the entire human race, throughout space.

I also wanted to send a message: "Help! My boyfriend left me and I don't like my job and my best friend is so busy that I hardly see her and I feel awkward and unattractive and I'm lonely and I want someone to share my life with."

Instead I browsed Facebook and Instagram for a bit. Then, I read a bunch of random articles : the sexiest celebrities in bikinis; actresses with their babies; a girl who had gone from from 110 to 60 kilos because her face sort of looked like yours. You should see the before and after pictures. By the way, Angelina, I remember, a few months before you and Brad announced your separation, I was surprised by how thin you were. Then I read that Brad was worried because you weighed just 43 kilos. Something I didn't know: that you were super jealous! That comforted me a little, not because I don't want what's best for you—of course not!—but because I realized that things are not always what they appear to be.

Next I looked up apartments for rent. Living with my mother and, intermittently, Cesar had become unbearable. I was 45 years old and dreamed of having an apartment all to myself. At one point David had even considered living together, in a place we both liked, this house 50 kilometers from Madrid. We took a virtual tour of the property, which looked like a ranch from an old Western movie. David and I both loved the countryside, the wild and open landscapes, free from the hustle and bustle of the city.

Looking at the photos of that ranch I imagined the happy life of a couple at one with nature. Ridiculous! Some couple we were—me, who has never left my neighborhood of Usera, and David, who hasn't traveled much of the world either. Yet when we imagined our life together, we thought of a wooden house in the middle of the wooded countryside, a river running through it and snow-capped mountains in the distance. We'd ride around in his SUV or on horseback. Then, in the late afternoon, we would have a drink on the porch in front of the yellow meadows and the oak trees illuinated by the last rays of sunlight. He would wear a Ralph Lauren plaid shirt and country boots with spurs, like John Wayne.

My cell phone rang and a picture of Vanessa flashed on the screen, dressed like she was going to a party. I closed my computer and lay down on the couch with my phone in my hand. It had been a long time since we'd seen each other and we'd arranged to meet that night at a bar near my house.

***

When she sat down across from me, a couple of feet away from the noisy bar, she was more serious than usual.

"It's been a long time since we've seen each other," I said.

"I've been really busy," she said. "But actually, well, I really wanted to tell you something. I hope you're not upset. Neither of us wanted to hurt you.

"David," I said.

Deep down, I'd always known.

"I wanted to tell you in person. At first—"

"Don't worry," I cut her off. "It's not necessary."

The waiter came over to take our order.

"Sorry, I have to go," I said to the waiter. "I'm late for an appointment."

Vanessa also stood up.

"I'm really sorry," she said. "Don't you want to talk? I understand that you're angry."

"I'm not angry," I said. "Besides, lately I've been thinking that, deep down, he and I didn't have all that much in common. Don't worry about me, I have other friends."

"I'd like to see you again sometime. I don't want things to end like this."

"Of course, I'll see you around," I said, "I hope it goes well!"

I'm happy to report that I didn't cry. I took my headphones out of my bag and plugged them into my phone. I didn't feel like going home so I decided to take a walk around the neighborhood. I cued up Mozart's Piano Concerto No. 21, which by now I knew well.

On the street commuters were hurrying back to their homes after a long day's work at their various, precarious jobs. Sooner or later death would catch up with them. It was natural selection. The buildings lined up along the streets looked so ugly to me—strange that I hadn't noticed them until now. A neighborhood built by unscrupulous builders for people with no great prospects for the future. They represented the filth and the burden of our lives: mine, mom's, César's; always counting every euro, manically disguising everything with a tacky lavishness. Not even the beauty of the José Hierro Library could compensate for so much ugliness. It bore the name of a poet that almost nobody had read. I also liked the church and the park and the 6 Bus, which took me directly to Atocha and downtown to do my shopping.

I didn't feel like going home and submitting to Mom's interrogation, so I decided to take the opportunity to go buy some shampoo and hair straightener. Chinatown was just waking up with its lanterns and colors and smells.

I returned hoe with my Chinatown shopping bags in hand. I heard some noises from mom's room—she was probably taking off her makeup. She'd always followed the same beauty ritual. I heard the sound of her shoes falling to the floor. The wall between us was like paper. I slipped into bed without making a sound.

Chapter 11
Varieties of Wolves

When I returned to the residence the next day, I went to Don Ramiro's room. Luckily, he was alone. His skin was blue, his terrible suffering reflected in his face. He couldn't no longer holding up his head, which was tilted to the right like a limp flower. He had been given a feeding tube, because he was unable to eat by himself, and his inert hands could not even turn the pages of the girly magazine I'd given him. Still he smiled at me. How much time would he have left—a month? Two? He could barely make a sound; only signs and glances. Finally I understood—he wanted to know if I had gotten the prescription for him that I'd taken from his drawer.

"I've been really busy with personal stuff, but I promise you that tomorrow I will go to the pharmacy and get it. Don't worry."

He looked at me with a look that reminded me of the poodle Mon and I used to have, when we already knew she was going to die and she spent her last days curled up on her pillow. I took his hand to say goodbye. The supervisor had called me into her office.

She greeted me grimly. In the past month, my coworkers had complained about my lack of dedication at work. According to them, I spent most of my time in the bathroom or in the cafeteria and they had to cover for me. She had no choice but to inform management. I felt totally indifferent to the words of this woman, who spoke to me her mouth puckered as if she were sucking a lemon. In any case, they wouldn't have renewed my contract, even I had been the second coming of Florence Nightingale. I didn't care; I wanted to change jobs. It was already clear to me that I had no vocation as a caregiver. I had to find another way to live!

The doorbell of Room 220 rang. I opened the door and heard a shrill voice.

—Come, come. There's no one here to take care of me. They leave me alone all day long."

I approached Ramona's bed and noticed the bracelet she was holding between her rheumatically twisted fingers. In the darkness, the bracelet had a warm glow as if it were made of real gold. I yanked it off her. The old woman snatched it back from me, closing her deformed hand over the precious metal.

"Let me see your bracelet for a second."

I tried to calm her down and spread her fingers. She screamed, a high-pitched squeal, and I covered her mouth with my hand in fright. I heard someone open the door and almost started to scream myself. Luckily, it was Marta. I sighed in relief. She was my only ally among my callous coworkers.

"I was just trying to look at her jewelry," I said. "What do you think of it?"

Marta approached us and, with a few caresses, got Ramona to let go of her bracelet. Then she went through the rest of her belongings. The door opened again. Didn't anybody knock? It was Tania.

"Is something wrong? I thought I heard a noise."

While Tania was talking, Marta was calmly putting Ramona's trinkets in order and returning them to her closet. In that moment I admired her.

"Ramona was a little nervous today and didn't want to take her medication, but now she's going to be good, right?" she said, looking at Tania with an accomplice smile.

The old lady smiled. Marta certainly had a way with old people.

"Come on!" she gave Ramona some medicine. "You have to take what the doctor prescribed."

Marta and I left the residence together. I carried Ramona's bracelet in my purse. Marta knew a pawn shop on Main Street where they bought gold and silver. We agreed to go there the next Saturday morning.

My intuition hadn't failed me: They gave us a thousand euros in bills for the bracelet. Now I think, Angelina, that maybe it doesn't seem right to you, but I want to be honest with you and look—I don't regret it! I understand if you don't want to hear from me anymore.

I'm sorry! But poor Ramona could no longer enjoy her jewelry, she had lost her mind, no one had visited her in the last five years and it would have eventually, undoubtedly, ended up in worse hands than ours. We weren't hurting anyone. In any case, from then on Marta and I would go to see Ramona in her room more often, treating her with a kindness and familiarity that sweetened her last days. For all my faults, Angelina, I am not ungrateful.

***

When we left the pawn shop, Marta and I went to look at stores in Salamanca. First we went into Zadig & Voltaire and tried on a few things. She looked great in everything with that great body of hers. She reminded me of Vanesa. Then we went to Armani. A nosy sales clerk greeted me effusively. Somehow, her feigned cheerfulness comforted me and made me feel more confident, as if my presence actually provoked some genuine enthusiasm.

"Does she know you? -Marta asked me, surprised.

Then I told her that, when he was still mobile, Don Ramiro and I would go shopping here. Now his family was doing everything possible to keep him isolated.

She was pensive for a moment. I tried on a t-shirt and Marta tried on a pair of jeans. Then we went into a pub, which had a huge plasma TV showing soccer games. We ordered beers. There were other customers euphorically and noisily participating in the sports revelry. We split what was left of the bracelet money; I put it in a fanny pack and Marta in her pants pocket. My new friend and I were having fun like little girls.

"What are you doing this weekend?" she asked.

"I don't know yet."

"I'm in this band, we play on Saturday night at a place on Libertad Street. Come."

I accepted the invitation and Marta accompanied me to the subway.

"Have you ever been married?" she asked.

"Not yet," I answered.

"Me, twice."

"And how did it go?"

"At first great, then bad. The end, in both cases, was awful. How about you?"

"With my last boyfriend it started out wonderful, then he disappeared."

"Well, that's just as well! You doged a bullet."

"There are plenty of people who in happy relationships."

"Who knows what will happen when you roll the dice again. For now we both feel free. I'm glad we're in the same boat."

I returned home with several packages—my bipolar side, my shrink would later say. Mom had gone out with César. I hadn't realized how tired I was: I lay down on the bed in my clothes and fell asleep right away. In my dreams, I went back to our old apartment, the one we had before Mom and I moved to Usera, when the whole family lived together. When I woke up, I tried to remember: did the bedroom that Lara and I shared have wallpaper? Yes, turquoise floral wallpaper and white twin beds.

The next day I had an afternoon shift, so in the morning I went to El Globo Pharmacy.

"This prescription is out of date. Wait here a moment," said the middle-aged man at the counter. The pharmacist disappeared into the back room. He returned within a minute.

"I can't make prepare this prescription for you. Apart from the fact that it is very difficult to obtain the main ingredienct, it would be illegal," he told me. "Batracotoxin is a very dangerous substance, comes from the skin of a frog found in Colombia. Who gave you this prescription?

"An elderly gentleman," I answered. "He had it in his house for a long time."

"It is not exactly a medicine—it's one of the most lethal poisons in existence. Indigenous tribes used this powder to coat their arrows. It can also be used for some medical preparations, but we can't do that here. And you don't know what he wants it for?"

"He has a house in the country and there are a lot of rats and mice," I thought to say.

"Well, then you've got the wrong store. Go to a grocery store, they usually sell rat poison there. Or Amazon."

I called Enrique.

"How are you doing, Angelina? I'm so glad you called me. Tell me, how is our friend doing?" he asked.

"Bad, suffering a lot. His nephews are there all the time now. I don't know why, they never visited him before. But I'm calling to tell you that the prescription Don Ramiro wants them to prepare for him isn't available."

"Don't worry, Angelina. I'll give you something similar for you to take with you, the only important thing is that you don't tell anyone that you've talked to me or that I've been to the residence. Whoever asks you, you don't know me at all, you don't know who I am, okay?"

"Okay."

After talking to Enrique, I felt a sense of relief. He was the kind of person that you know you can trust.

Chapter 12
Nature of Instincts

There are things that are beautiful for the
simple fact of not being able to possess them.

Gilgamesh

The following week, no one at the residence scold me again. I only had a month left on my contract anway and it was clear that they were not going to renew it. I didn't really care. I take everything as it comes—I've always believed in fate. I went to Chinatown to buy some pastries and took them to Ramona. She was very happy when she saw me. She seemed to recognize me and even squeezed my hand when I said goodbye.

In hospice, Don Ramiro's family took turns never to leave him alone. If I wanted to visit him, it was under the watchful eye of one of his two nephews and the Belgian woman, who I hated most of all. Generally, residents in Don Ramiro's situation were allowed to go to another hospice or to his own home for this last stretch of their life. But his nephews, who after having gone so long without seeing him would not leave his side, had managed to keep him in Valdeluz.

I felt more and more burdened with work. At night, when I got home exhausted, my only distraction was to go on my computer in the solitude of my room.

My time on the internet allowed me to escape my real life and to feel satisfied with the life that I projected in the virtual world. Since I was a teenager, I've struggled to achieve anything that mattered. My mother valued the same things as all the other housewives in the neighborhood: a good job, a good boyfriend, a body that looked like a soap opera star. I wish a fairy godmother could have waved her wand and given it all to me. I wanted to feel as appreciated admired as you must feel, Angelina. I longed for something more than the drab, bland life of my parents, but now here, in this hospital bed, I think those desires were illusory and a bit selfish. There's this line from David's favorite videogame, called *Inferno* or something—what fun we both had playing that and other videogames in his beautiful house in Aravaca! Those were the good old days when I admired him and he had not yet become a that ridiculous wannabe executive who came to visit me the other day. Anyway, there's this line in the game: "Humans are creatures of desire, they cannot exist without wanting something. To what extent do you appreciate that desire, here, in the academy of hell?

This quote came to mind because this hospital is also a bit like the academy of hell. Desires here are more basic: to be free of pain, to live a little longer, a feel little better. The desire to eat disappears. For me, I was hungriest when I most wanted to lose weight.

At the hospital, you can't use the computer. Back around the time I knew that my contract at Valdeluz was not going to be renewed, I started to spend a lot of time in front of my computer. There I could chat with people and enjoy a space where happiness felt within reach. A happiness that was banal, perhaps, but colorful, possible, and, moreover, free. On Matching Friends, I didn't have to pay for moments of happiness, unlike when, in real life, I went on a trip or went shopping. But the best thing was that online I could make money.

Not like Vanesa did, as an influencer with her website and her thousands of Instagram followers that she managed to monetize by getting brands to pay her for talking about their products. In my case, it seems that having virtual relationships with strangers is one of the few things I am gifted at. When I started photoshopping my pics to look hotter, and letting my suitors' imagination run wild, their number and payment solvency, by card or PayPal, started increasing right away. It's pretty easy, Angelina, even for an average-looking girl me.

I'm ashamed to tell you, Angelina, and I hope you forgive me, that I used your body once, the body I wished I had, and added my face to it in Photoshop.

On Matching Friends, there was no foreplay—anyone who paid the two-euro membership fee already knew what they were getting into. I could have virtual sex simultaneously with a guy from Detroit, a guy in Melbourne, and a guy in Hamburg, all at the same time. I learned how to spot catfishes and, best of all, how to monetize my skills as a source of income.

The truth is that I ended up becoming a virtuoso of online relationships. I'm won't go into details, but I spent almost all my free time on the Internet.

I advertised with my name, Angelina Fernández, and slogans like "Virtual sex burns calories" or "Improve your endurance with online sex", "Sex without the risk."

Imagine, Angelina! Me—the useless, clumsy, bland Mari Pili—was one the calling the shots. I began to feel more self-confident and to improve my self-esteem. There were people, mostly men, who admired me, sought me out and paid to hang out with me virtually. I began to realize that there were lots of great things about me—it was just that, as Marta had said, many people were too stupid to appreciate them.

On Matching Friends and other similar sites I've lived the lives of many people. I've had sex, yes, a lot of sex, sex as good as David and I had, but less painful because here, in my virtual life, I'm free from sorrow, from nostalgia, from all affliction. I finally had a job that I liked and with which I might be able to earn enough to live on! It was just a matter of dedicating time to it.

As it happens, spending my free hours in front of the computer actually helped me save money. I like to interact with men online, but for shopping I need a more sensual experience: touching the fabric of a dress, smelling the aroma of a store, chatting up the salesclerks. Buying clothes online is like having a sugar-free dessert—unsatisfying. Now during my free time, instead of going out to shop and spend money, I could be paid to sit at home.

***

That afternoon a package arrived for me at home. There was no return address, but I immediately knew who it was from. Inside the cardboard box were two pairs of disposable plastic gloves, a dosing bottle, and a piece of paper with instructions. That night, shift change was at 9:30, so I Don Ramiro would be alone then. I went to his room and asked him if he was sure he wanted to do this. He nodded his head. I said goodbye to him and grabbed his hand. He faintly smiled and closed his eyes. I poured the drops into a glass of water and added a plastic lid and a straw that I had on the bedside table. I gave it to him to drink while holding his head with my other hand. Through the plastic gloves I could feel the last of the warmth on the skin of his neck.

No one saw me enter or leave. I remembered Enrique Gallardo's words: "You don't know who I am, you've never seen me." Now I didn't know who the old man in 323 was either, just a number, soon to be passed on to another resident.

Chapter 13
Rats Supplanting
Each Other

> You often meet your fate on the
> path you took to avoid it.
>
> THE GOOD QUEEN

When I went upstairs the next morning, I met Tania, who came up to me and said quietly:

"Did you hear that tonight Don Ramiro was found dead in his bed? Leila went into his room and he wasn't breathing."

Tania seemed scared and excited at the same time. For the first time since I started working at Valdeluz, she spoke to me in a friendly way.

"Now the whole family is at the morgue," she added.

"Do you know which morgue?" I asked.

"The one next to the San Isidro Cemetery."

When our shift was over, Marta and I went to the morgue. Although it was winter, it was sunny. From the entrance, which was on a hill, we could see a beautiful park with bright green treetops, the cemetery surrounded by a stone wall, and Madrid in the distance. The room where the Don Ramiro'd was being looked like Room 323. Having Marta there calmed me down. I noticed Enrique standing next to Don Ramiro's family, but I didn't approach him. Remembering his instructions, I hardly looked at him. I did, however, offer my condolences to the old man's nephews and their wives, who thanked me coldly.

Two days later, Tania gave me the news of Don Ramiro's death again, this time with more detail. The doctor on duty had certified a natural death, heart failure due to his age and poor health. But there was a complication.

"They still haven't buried him," Tania said. "His nephews want an autopsy and have filed a complaint for the judge to authorize it. Don't tell anyone I told you!"

The next day at the residence, the atmosphere felt different than usual. My coworkers were huddling around and talking to each other. Apparently, the supervisor had said that Don Ramiro's nephews wanted an investigation to be launched. The idea of an investigation frightened me. What if I was questioned by the police? What if I had left behind fingerprints? Had I been too hasty in doing this for Don Ramiro, without stopping to think about the consequences it could have for me? I had been reckless and crazy and all because I wanted to help him, Angelina. But what did I have to gain from his death?

Both the staff and the residents were in shock. All sorts of options were being discussed, some of them truly macabre. Fortunately, no one was paying attention to me, so I took the opportunity go get a massage and a facial at the spa nextdoor. When I returned after an hour and a half, no one had noticed my absence.

At the end of our day, Marta and I went to dinner at an Italian restaurant with the money we had left over from pawning Ramona's bracelet. I was scared and came clean with her.

"Please don't say anything," I said. "Do you think they'll put me in jail?"

She reassured me that she'd had also been on the night shift the day of Don Ramiro's death. The management had roped off his suite—no one was allowed in, in case it was a crime scene.

The idea of the police looking for possible signs of an assisted suicide—that's what Tania called it—made me shudder. The results of the autopsy, which would establish the precise time of the old man's death, were not yet known. From what Tania had told me, suspicions of who could have helped him to die would likely on someone who had worked the night shift that day. It was all just a matter of speculation. "The poor guy must have been just laying there stiff as a board for hours," Tania had said to me. This turn of events had brought out a kindness in her that I'd never known before.

Marta ordered ravioli and I ordered osso buco.

"You know I've found a better job?" said Marta.

She was thinking of leaving Valdeluz and had an offer from a real estate agency to show houses. She would get a commission for each apartment she sold, but he also would have a fixed salary, though it wasn't very high. She'd already started doing some work for them.

"I have a new job too," I said. "It's on the Internet."

"You're an influencer?"

"Something like that≥ I develop content for a company."

"Oh, I know! The metaverse, right? I have a friend with a degree in advertising and marketing and she works at Facebook, doing stuff with the metaverse.

"Yes, that's right. The metaverse."

"I like real estate," said Marta. "Selling houses, you meet a lot of interesting people. You see how people live and you get to move around instead of being stuck in an office." Hey, let's toast to our new jobs," she said.

We clinked our glasses of wine and then had two more. I could see all my fears about Don Ramiro's death fading away in the distance. For dessert we each ordered a cappuccino.

The coffee had sobered me up a bit, but when I got home I took a nap. My mother had gone out with César for the afternoon and a strange silence permeated the apartment. When I woke up, the effect of the drinks had worn off and I was afraid again. It was Wednesday, the day I had dinner with Dad. I walked to his house to get some exercise. Better not than staying home alone, anguished, thinking about the possibility that I might end up being implicated in the poor old man's death. And of course I didn't dare call Enrique for help.

Dad had bought salad, smoked salmon, and a turkey and tomato sandwich for me.

"I brought you things I know you like and that are not fattening. And for dessert, no sugar: a kiwi and a yogurt."

"Thank you."

"How's work? Are they finally going to renew your contract?"

"Don't worry, Dad. I got a better job."

"A better job?"

-Yes, on the Internet. I'm working on content for the metaverse."

The truth was that, in addition to Matching Friends, I started participating in chats on other erotic dating sites. Except for Tinder, where monetization was not possible, in the rest I got money from advertisers based on the amount of time users spent chatting with me and the number of times they repeated the search for my name or pseudonym. In addition to the analysis of their profiles that they obtained through *cookies.* Marta had hit the nail on the head with the metaverse, it was the ideal word to find a way to define my work. Marta always so smart!

"And it's legal?" Dad asked me.

"Yes, Dad, totally legal."

"And do they pay well?"

"Yes, it's great. A lot more money than the nursing home."

"But Valdeluz still seems more secure. These new fads always come with risks. I mean, I don't even know what the metaverse is."

"Imagine, for example, that you're paralyzed," I said. "You put on a pair of glasses and the can assign yourself an avatar to live a virtual life where you can walk again."

"I don't like to imagine that kind of thing. I have enough to deal with in real life. I don't want to know anything about avatars. I wish you had a permanent job at a serious company. You know, Angelina, now that I'm about to cash in my retirement fund, I was thinking of lending you some money to put a down payment on an apartment. At your age, it's about time you owned an apartment."

"I'd love to buy an apartment in Pozuelo or Aravaca."

"That's a bit pricy— better to buy an apartment here in Usera."

Dad didn't understand that living in Aravaca was not the same as living in Parla or Usera, just like being a metaverse content marketing director—thank goodness I'd come up with a name for my new job—was not the same as wiping asses in an old people's home. Dad had always had very limited ambitions.

"Don't worry, Dad. I'll buy wherever I can afford."

"You're not eating anything—don't you like it?"

"I'm not hungry."

It was true. Every time I thought about some medical examiner doing an autopsy of poor Don Ramiro, my stomach sank. Tomorrow I would call Enrique. I had to talk to him.

Chapter 14
Birds Incapable of Flight

I had only a week of work left and every day I felt more anguished. Nobody spoke again about the autopsy results, but Room 323 was still closed off. Every day I searched online and in newspapers for reports on Don Ramiro's death, but it seemed to have gone unnoticed by the press. I only found an obituary in *ABC* that had been sent in by his nephews.

On Thursday, with only one day left of work and a plan to sleep until noon before my afternoon shift, Mom woke me up banging on my bedroom door and yelling.

"You have a call from the notary's office!"

I got up, combing my hair with my hand, and walked over to the landline in the living room.

"Are you Angelina Fernández Peinado?" said a voice. "We are calling you from the notary's office of Mr. Enrique Gallardo. Please wait a moment, the notary wants to talk to you."

"Good morning, Angelina." It was Enrique. I wanted to inform you that your name has appeared in Ramiro Téllez de Velarde's last will and testament. He leaves you a sum of money for the good care you took of him at the end of his life. I will now hand you over to my secretary, who will make an appointment for you to come and sign, if you accept the bequest."

Mom insisted on accompanying me to the notary's office, even planning the clothes she planned to wear—a gray suit jacket—but I put my foot down. My mother was fascinated by all the places she considered of high standing and a notary's office was one of them, plus she was curious to know what awaited her daughter. A behavior that my shrink would later define as a tendency toward overprotection, possibly due to Lara's accident, which made her still see me as a child.

"I prefer to go alone, thank you," I said. She looked at me with reproach.

The office was in an old and stately building on Alfonso XII Street. It was decorated like the English *country clubs* I've seen on TV, to which you already know, Angelina, I am also addicted. On the wood-paneled walls hung pictures of racehorses and some oil paintings of country landscapes. After a few minutes in the waiting room, a secretary asked for my ID and escorted me to another room with a dark wooden table in the center that gleamed as if it had been freshly waxed. After 15 minutes, Enrique arrived, dressed dapperly. Only when he smiled at me with that same smile I'd first seen in the hallway of Valdeluz did I calm down. He was accompanied by a man who introduced himself as an officer of the notary's office and a woman who handed Enrique some papers.

The notary explained to me that, in his will, Don Ramiro had left me one hundred and fifty thousand euros, on which I would have to pay income tax. More than joy, I felt a kind of dizziness.

I could not imagine myself with that kind of money. Instead of feeling celebratory I felt insecure. When I went shopping with Don Ramiro, I never saw a penny—he always discreetly ordered the bills to be charged to his account with a barely perceptible gesture. The fancier the place is, the less hard cash you see. It's not like in my neighborhood Chinatown, where you see guys clutching their fanny pack straps as if they're going to be robbed at a moment's notice. I managed to pull myself together and ask:

"And when will the money be available to me?"

Enrique gave an impish smile that made him look younger.

"As soon as the paperwork is finished, a couple of months at the most. I don't think any of the heirs will object and start probate proceedings."

I wondered if the will had something to do with the paper he took from Don Ramiro's suite.

"It turns out that our friend made a new will shortly before he died," Enrique told me. "In the previous one, all his money was for his next of kin, but at the last moment he decided to change it and gave me the new one. He has left the money to be distributed to ornithological society charities and a few mandates, including yours. His nephews and nieces will receive nothing."

Then the notary proceeded to read aloud Don Ramiro's will, in which bequeathed me one hundred and fifty thousand euros in gratitude for my care. When Enrique finished reading, I was handed back my ID and shown where to sign.

When the officer and the secretary left, I approached Enrique.

"I'm really scared," I told him. "What if they see he left me all this money and accuse me of murdering him? I heard that the autopsy found some substance in his blood that breathing to fail."

"They'll probably just find traces of tramadol, an opiate that in large doses can cause death."

I thought that if Enrique knew the result of the autopsy it was because he himself had provided me with the medicine for Don Ramiro. I was crazy to trust an anonymous and unknown sender. Although don Ramiro had expressed to me his desire to leave, I should have thought about the consequences it could have for me.

I started to cry.

"Then I'm done for. They'll investigate and put me in jail. They'll think that I gave him the medicine to get that money. And it's not true—I didn't know anything about this will!"

"Don't worry, Angelina. Nothing is going to happen to you. Trust me."

"But what if the police question me?"

"Calm down, that's not going to happen."

"But how do you know? I heard that the police are going to go to Valdeluz to interrogate everyone who were there the night Don Ramiro died."

"Angelina, if anything happens to you, just call me. You already have my phone number. I'll make sure they can't accuse you of anything."

I said goodbye to Enrique. My head was boiling in a sea of confusion of conflicting emotions.

The next day at work—perhaps it was my paranoia—it seemed to me that all my coworkers knew about the inheritance. I sensed hostility in every glance. But no one spoke to me about him again, except Tania, who seemed to be staying on top of things. She told me she had heard that Don Ramiro's nephews wanted his uncle's will to be declared null and void, because they thought that the old man had been manipulated, his illness taken advantage of, and that he was not mentally fit to sign anything. Tania's words left me in a state of shock, but I kept working like an automaton. Monday finally arrived, with no further news about the death of Don Ramiro Téllez de Velarde. Room 323 was still sealed off.

I went up to the secretary's office and the personnel manager gave me an envelope with my last paycheck.

That night, Marta and I went together to a concert at El Intruso, a bar on Augusto Figueroa Street. I didn't pay much attention to the performances or to what Marta explained to me was cutting-edge funk pop—I could only think about what would happen if the police discovered that I had been responsible for Don Ramiro's death. I had two glasses of gin, one after the other. When I returned home, in Marta's car, a little dizzy, I felt like I was on a swing, like when my mother used to take us to Pradolongo park after school. I as afraid I'd fall over.

"In three months I'll finally have a rich friend," Marta said as she dropped me off.

I could forget about all my crappy contract and bitchy colleagues at Valdeluz. Besides, her real estate business was starting to take off. The future was ours.

Mom, on the other hand, was pushing me to buy an apartment instead of wasting my money on something frivolous. Now that I could afford a mortgage, I had to make the most of it and put a down payment on an apartment. The idea that you had to have your own apartment to be somebody in life was one of the few things she shared with Dad.

Every day she would read the ads in the newspaper sections and bring me catalogs of new housing developments.

"If you don't mind, since I know you don't have much time, I'll help you look," she said, handing me a brochure for a house with a terrace and a view and a gym.

The search for my apartment had become part of her daily routine. That future apartment became a kind of talisman of happiness. She'd start the day by reading *Idealist* to see if there was anything new on the market. Then began the calls to make an appointment with the real estate agents, which usually happened when she finished work.

"I have a friend who works in real estate," I told Mom. "She knows my tastes."

"Well, that's great," she said. "I think we should focus our search in our neighborhood—the houses here are getting much more valuable."

"I want to live in an apartment with a communal garden in Pozuelo or Aravaca," I told her.

"That's going to be too expensive," she said, twisting his face, "and you're going to have to ask the bank for a mortgage that you won't be able to pay later. It's a mistake to go into that kind of lifelong debt."

She agreed with Dad on that, too.

She never said anything about it to me, but I wondered if my mother had heard rumors that my relationship with Don Ramiro had gone beyond my work as a caregiver. The suspicion that someone might question my integrity cross my mind like a shadow amid the stream of videos and photos of real estate bargains that she showed me every morning.

Chapter 15
Erratic Songs
in the Azores

This is our story, let's finish it together.

Final Fantasy x

Freed from working at the residence, I started dedicating my days to my new job online. Especially, since I discovered Matching Friends, which was not only a networking site, but also gave the opportunity to get money. "If you are looking for friendships or just to meet people with the same interests as you, then this site is your best option," said the site's advertisement. But the most interesting thing was the facilities it provided for monetizing contacts. Created in Saint-Tropez, this application pays the user for dating another person. At first, I didn't understand how it worked until I understood what it was: an *app* created to earn money for dating strangers.

It's simple. First you register; then you fill out your bio names and upload a photo of yourself. Finally, you can choose among all the registered users who you want to chat with. If you meet up with him or her, you can choose between several available plans: going out for a coffee, five euros; going to the movies, ten euros; having a drink, fifteen euros; or eating in a restaurant, thirty-five euros; traveling to another city, between one hundred and one thousand euros. Those are the rates of Matching Friends, but there are others that allow for encounters entirely online. The rates are much lower, you can make a lot more appointments. And the best part is you don't have to leave your house.

Then something happened—I fell in love again. Or, at least, I started to. As soon as I saw Bruno's picture, I knew it was really him and not a catfish. Bruno is the kind of guy who carries his masculinity with discretion. Classy, not an exhibitionist. And the truth, Angelina, is that I was fed up with metrosexuals, freaks, and tacky beach bums. Bruno had brown hair, blue eyes, dressed in Ralph Lauren. In the winter he might add a Uniqlo vest. He kept it simple. Best of all, he chose me. Now I just want to talk about him, not the legion of guys who paid just to talk to me, who used Matching Friends to live out their erotic fantasies.

Believe it or not, Angelina, since starting my new job I also became addicted to reading. I devoured literature, bestsellers, self-help, celebrity memoirs. In school, my intelligence had been determined by a test to be "below-average," but I like to write, even if it is the kind of low-quality prose you find online. Something changed for me when I realized that, with my imagination, I could control my reality.

***

Mom was screaming for me, as usual.
"Run, Angelina, run! Come!"

Mom and Cesar are the kind of people who can't stand to be quiet. Sometimes I think they should spend a vacation in a Carthusian monastery to learn that human beings can spend whole stretches of time without uttering a sound.

"Look! They are talking about the Valdeluz residence on a TV gossip show!"

A journalist interviewed Enrique, who said that he was solely responsible for having given Don Ramiro the solution that caused his death. It had been a mutual agreement with him to end his suffering.

The camera focused on the document that Enrique had handed to the host of the program. I don't think I have ever seen Enrique without some paper in his hand. He explained to the journalist, it was the living will of Ramiro Téllez de Velarde. His elderly friend had called him to ask for his help and to leave a record of his desire to put an end to his suffering. He left him in charge of choosing the way to end his life. After the host had read the document, the notary handed her a second piece of paper in which the old man, fifteen days after having signed his living will, ratified his decision to have him help him die. Although at that time a euthanasia law was being drafted in Spain, it had not yet been presented to the Congress of Deputies, so Enrique Gallardo's action could be considered illegal, the program host explained to the viewers.

Enrique assumed full responsibility. He even implied that he himself had administered the medicine, saying that he had been with him at nine o'clock in the evening, ten minutes before I came to see him.

At that moment a Pro-Life organization was tweeting at the program expressing their disagreement. For the first time in a long time, I felt free.

When the interview was over, I told Mom I had to work and went back to Matching Friends. Bruno had paid for the equivalent of a virtual coffee to chat with me. What I liked most about him was that he never started conversations by talking about anything sex-related or obscene, like other users did.

Bruno. How are you feeling today, beautiful?

Me. – I'm alright. Just got some good news.

Bruno: I'd like to give you some more good news, then.

Me: Hit me.

Bruno: I want to get to know you better. You have everything that I look for in a woman.

Me: But we've barely even chatted.

Bruno: Do you like classical music?

Me: Yes. I'm a huge Mozart fan.

Bruno: I knew it. He's my favorite too. I want to travel with you.

Me: Where to?

Bruno: We could start in Vienna. Have you ever been?

Me: No.

Bruno: Well, then, perfect: Vienna, Mozart, and Angelina.

88

Me: Okay, Bruno, we'll talk about it next time. I think we're running out of time for coffee.

Bruno: But we just started talking.

Me: The coffee chat option doesn't give us much time. Tomorrow I'll find us better option.

Bruno: All right. In the meantime, think of Vienna, Mozart, and me.

I had a lot more time left to chat with Bruno, but something made me want to cut things short. Sometimes, happiness can be as devastating as sorrow—you have to know how to dose it so that it doesn't overtake you completely. After Enrique had freed me from my guilt, my intuition urged me not to look into the abyss.

Bruno played another kind of music that let the imagination work. There would be time for the rest... I've never been a fan of skipping steps. Mozart! At least David had left me with something good. Now I could think of him without resentment.

Chapter 16
The Domestic Instinct

I feel like-if-I could, like I could... conquer the world.

Day of the tentacle (video game)

Sometimes Bruno and I videochatted. He was sitting in a garden in front of a teak table, while I chose a neutral background and a flattering filter.

"This is the garden at my house," he explained. "I like to live surrounded by trees. And you, Angelina, where are you?"

"At the moment I'm staying with my mother, but I'm going to buy an apartment soon."

"Have you already thought about where?"

"Yes, north of Madrid: Aravaca, Pozuelo, or Majadahonda."

"You must have a good job."

"I just received a family inheritance."

"I've been thinking about our trip to Austria. Do you know what a walkabout is?"

Bruno explained to me that the Aboriginals in Australia, when they get older, have to make a long journey before they can return to their village and are accepted by the community. They go off on their own, cross the great Australian outback and then travel to many different places and get to know the world before returning home again. It is a kind of initiation journey, a test of their survival skills that they have to pass before becoming adults.

"I'm an adult," I told hi.

"You can always learn and mature, it doesn't matter how old you are. The important thing is to have an adventure or discover something you don't know about the world."

"But aren't you saying that to do the walkabout you have to travel alone?"

"You can also do the walkabout accompanied. There's lots we could discover together."

"We could start by taking a virtual tour to get to know each other better," I said.

"Ha ha ha! You're so funny, Angelina. The Aboriginals didn't have internet. Besides, I'd rather see your beautiful face in person. Can you imagine what it would be like to explore the world as an avatar, with all that metaverse bullshit? Primitive tribes were in touch with nature and sought to overcome the obstacles that must be faced when we travel without money or comforts. In short, to prepare us for life. Tell me, besides Austria, where else would you like to go?"

"Sometimes I think I'd like to live on a ranch."

"I have a friend who has a ranch in the Rocky Mountains. We can visit him."

Bruno was the kind of guy who had friends everywhere.

"That would be very nice. But what I wanted was to buy a little place to spend summers or weekends."

"You're unbelievable, Angelina! I thought you wanted to buy an apartment in Aravaca? Look, if we end up being a couple, we'll have that ranch. I'm an architect and I like to build houses. I'll build one for both of us."

"Okay, but first we'll have to do our walkabout."

"You get me. You're so beautiful, inside and out. I've already told you, when I talk to you, I think you're what I've always been looking for."

I always learn something when I'm with Bruno—something I haven't experienced since David. Bruno's family must have money, by what I could see of his house in the background of our video call, and by the number of places he's been and the important people he namedrops with whom he's rubbed shoulders. From the way he talks and writes and dresses, you can tell he had a good education. When we chat, I always run my messages through a spellchecker. But I think that, in the end, both our abilities and our limitations come out somewhere. The doorbell rang. I said goodbye to Bruno and went to answer the door. It was two policemen.

"Are you Angelina Fernández Peinado?"

They were polite, which scared me even more. I nearly threw up my morning coffee. Just then Mom came in from the grocery store.

"Who is this?" she asked, still holding her shopping bags.

"Don't worry, ma'am," said one of the policemen. "We just want to talk to your daughter."

"But why?"

My mother turned to me and said quietly, "I'm sure it's something to do with that old man's inheritance. I knew it wasn't going to do you any good."

"Calm down, ma'am, please," the policeman interrupted.

I watched everything play out as if I was outside of my body, floating above our tiny living room. The tallest policeman, who looked at me like a cockroach he'd just found in the kitchen, identified himself and showed me a warrant to enter my mother's house, where I was registered as a resident. He added that I had the right not to make any statement without the presence of a lawyer.

The investigation that had led the two agents to our home was related to a lawsuit filed by a niece of Ramona Pérez Lastra, a resident of Valdeluz, during the time I was working there, for the theft of the old lady's jewelry.

Apparently, during her last visit to the nursing home, María Pérez Miró noticed a solid gold bracelet missing from her aunt's room. The Valdeluz Residence conducted an internal investigation, in the course of which one of the aides, Desiré López Rueda, stated that she had seen Ramona's bracelet in the pocket of my robe. According to her statement, one day she had seen me leaving Doña Ramona's room in a hurry. She followed me down the hallway. Suddenly, I sneezed and, as I reached into my pocket and took out a Kleenex, Desiré saw something glittering in the pocket of my white uniform. The policeman announced that I would have to go to the police station to make a statement.

When the two policemen closed the door of the house, Mom remained silent.

Chapter 17
Embryology and Development

People say they are on the wrong track
when it is simply by one's own path.

ANGELINA JOLIE

The first thing Mom did was to make an appointment with a psychiatrist recommended to her by her physician. Insurance paid for most of it, and she took care of the rest. Appearances were important to my mother; she was terrified that someone might find out what I was accused of and tarnish my reputation, and incidentally hers. Her Angelina accused of theft—an unacceptable blemish in her little world, which for her was the universe. That could not be—surely I was sick. She needed a professional explanation for my bout of kleptomania. Despite the fact that I had long since passed the age of majority, I agreed to visit Dr. Sergio Antunez.

once a week.

He wore round glasses and his hair thinned at his temples and the crown of his head. He listened to me with the kind of floating attention that Freud asked of psychoanalysts while I tried to make some sense of my vulgar life story. At our fifth session, we tried some free associations: mother-heavy; pleasure-buying; father-military uniform (that was a translation of dad's job as a sworn watchman); happiness-ranch. At the word "ranch" he first mentioned his theory: the ranch in my subconscious was a projection of my sexuality; I needed something solid to ground me in reality and give me security to hide what was deep inside me, a frigidity that prevented me from enjoying sex. My libido was dressed in the symbolism of nature and rugged testosterone. We continued.

Sex-field, perhaps because of the spring day when David and I were together for the first time in an abandoned hut.

Love-sadness. "Sadness. We have to go deeper into the meaning of that sadness," the doctor noted.

Money-theft.

"That association with theft is very interesting, we will analyze it later."

Sister-fear.

"Sister-fear! We'll see what it takes to get into fear," Sergio finally said. "Let's start there."

"I don't remember my sister," I said. "She died when she was five years old. For my parents, of course, it was a tragedy."

"And for you?"

"For me, too, I suppose, but I was only seven. Mom decided never to talk about her again. We hardly ever mentioned her name. I think it was a way to get over the pain."

"And did you miss her?"

"Yes, and at the same time I was glad that she had died and Mom could no longer compare me to her. The other night I dreamed that the two of us were together again."

"And what did you feel?"

"That I loved her. I cried and she consoled me and told me not to worry. That I wasn't to blame for anything, that I didn't hate her, that I didn't want her to disappear from the face of the earth."

"But why were you afraid of Lara? She was smaller than you, she couldn't hurt you. Surely it was fear of yourself, of the feelings she provoked in you, even if you were just a child."

"Maybe. Everyone liked me better than me. They would fawn over her: 'What a beautiful girl! What are you going to be when you grow up?' And I just stood there, silent.".

"So, you hated her."

"Sometimes."

"Only sometimes? Did you ever want her to die?

"Only sometimes."

Sergio looked at his watch.

"It's five o'clock. We have to conclude the session, but we'll come back to this next week."

I nodded. Although there was something arrogant about Sergio, he had a strange power over me.

Despite his greasy hair and his runaway chin, he dominated me mentally. One day I dreamt that he kissed me and, contrary to his theories about my frigidity, woke up burning with desire. In spite of everything, the analysis helped me to overcome the anguish and the feeling of failure that I had been dragging along. It was a matter of finding tools to gain self-confidence and forget the childish regression that made my relationship with my mother so infantile. I also had a love-hate relationship with her, which reproduced the one I had with Lara.

According to Dr. Antunez, it was the need to improve my physique at all costs that had driven me to steal. Apparently, I was unconsciously rejecting my ordinary appearance. I needed money to improve a body that I had rejected since childhood, when I was always compared to Lara. That's why I stole from an old lady who was in my care. I know what I did wrong, Angelina.

***

The doorbell rang. When I saw the mailman in his yellow uniform, I got a bad feeling.

"I bring a registered letter. You have to sign here," said the man.

It was a summons for a statement to the police. I tried to control my panic and called Emilio, Dad's lawyer friend. He'd offered to help me after the scare with Ramona's niece and the warrant for the police to search our home. Of course they didn't find anything—the five hundred euros I got for the bracelet were hanging in my closet as dresses.

I went to the police station with Emilio. The policeman asked me where I worked. When I told him that my job was in metadata content distribution, he asked me the name of the sites I worked for. When I mentioned Matching Friends, he smiled slightly.

"Content distributor, that's what they call it now," he mumbled.

Following Emilio's instructions, I denied the theft. I couldn't know what the old lady had done with her personal belongings, as there were many visitors to the residence. I limited myself to taking care of her and treating her with affection. The latter was true.

"I'd like to visit her at the residence, but I've been too busy lately."

"That's beside the point," said the policeman. "Besides, Doña Ramona has passed away. You can leave now. Don't forget to let us know if you are going to travel outside Spain."

Emilio accompanied me home and reassured me.

"Don't worry, Angelina. This case will come to nothing, you'll see. They don't have any evidence to convict you."

***

In my room I turned on my computer and logged on to Matching Friends.

BRUNO: How is my Scheherazade from Marcelo Usera?

I had told him where I lived. I already imagined he lived in Aravaca.

BRUNO: You look good in red.

He was wearing a white guayabera. I don't know why every posh guy I know wears a guayabera in the summer. Whatever, he looked gorgeous.

BRUNO. I am jealous of your fans.

Bruno and I, in addition to Matching Friends, where I used different pseudonyms so no one would know me, were friends on Facebook, where my profile was public.

BRUNO: I see that you get a lot of compliments every time you change your profile picture.

ME: Those are just the standard, polite comments that friends leave each other.

BRUNO: I can't help worrying someone might take it too far.

Me: Then I'll block them.

Bruno: I don't think anyone could be immune to your charm.

I sometimes spied on him on Facebook. I was so tormented by the competition from the other women that I would sometimes look through all the profile pictures of his Facebook friends.

Bruno: Did you receive what I sent you from the House of Music in Vienna? It's downtown, near St. Stephen's Square and a few steps from Mozart's house. It was the palace of Archduke Charles.

Me: Yes. I'll listen to Concerto No. 21 there.

Bruno: Do you play music when you're alone in your room before bed? My favorite singers are Lady Gaga, Rosalía, and Billie Eilish, in that order. What about you?

Me: Sometimes I go to concerts with my friend Marta. She likes underground clubs and improvised jazz. But I prefer, let me think... I like C. Tangana, Rozalén, and Raphael.

Bruno: Raphael?

Me: Yes, he was my dad's favorite. My dad used to play me his records when I was little—when he likes something he just plays it over and over again. From listening to it so much, I think I've grown fond of it.

Bruno: I can't wait to see you in person Angelina. Maybe if you hear me say it enough you'll end up getting a little bit fond of me too—love, love, love. I'd love to see you take off your red dress tonight.

Me. We'll have time for that later.

Deep down, I was afraid to meet faceto face. He'd find me much uglier than my photos. According to my shrink, I was beginning to reproduce in my virtual life the same fears and insecurities that plagued my real life. Bruno and I still didn't know each other physically, although I fantasized about him all the time. Now that I know a little about psychoanalysis, I know that the brain is the most sexual organ; in my brain there was only him. I could have virtual sex with a multitude of men, but Bruno was the only object of my fantasies. I spent my days in that mixture of reverie, eroticism, and loneliness that had long been part of my daily life.

***

My work on Matching Friends wasn't the only thing I did online, although it was the most secretive and the most lucrative. I also had my blog, my Facebook and my Instagram page about celebrities, fashion, and astrology, where I had amassed quite a following. Celebrity news is always popular. And the thing is, Angelina, I think it can be difficult for someone who has succeeded like you to understand the seduction that any manifestation of strength exerts on us, those who are part of the great army of the weak, the insecure, those who are always condemned to occupy the last places on the social ladder. People who are successful in something seem to us to be of a superior class to those of us who, like me, always feel several steps below what we would like. It has to do with what Sergio calls an inferiority complex.

I've always admired celebrities. I know it's silly, following people's lives just because they're on television, even if they don't do anything that interests us all that much. But you're different from other celebrities. I really admire you.

I only left the house to go to Sergio's office. I was very anxious after the police visit and, except for one time when I went shopping at the mall that had just opened in Usera, I spent the whole day in front of the computer chatting or having cybersex on Matching Friends.

Chapter 18
Inactive Summer
for Certain Animals

I am not crazy, my reality is different from yours.

ALICE IN WONDERLAND

I saw my shrink once a week. From my free associations, Sergio tried to understand the origin of my frigidity and everything else that was wrong with me.

"I was never frigid with David and now I'm in love with Bruno. I think about him all the time—I want him," I defended myself.

That was because I had never actually met him. Frigidity is characterized by only wanting what you can't have. And as for David, frigidity was at the heart of my relationship with him, even if I didn't realize it at the time. If I had continued seeing David, my shrink assured me, then my "true nature" would have come to the surface.

I became convinced that I just couldn't give David what he needed sexually, so it was no wonder he had abandoned me. But

I shouldn't feel guilty about it, Sergio insisted. Besides, clearly my frigidity was just one of many problems—we'd also have to address my bipolarity, my occasional bouts of kleptomania, and my penchants for virtual sex and luxury goods. The latter could be to compensate for my sexual dissatisfaction, a substitute for my lack of orgasms. It was clear that it was this latent frigidity, of which I had not been aware, that made me seek out online sex with strangersand take refuge in imaginary places like my dream ranch. But all this could be cured with the right psychotherapeutic treatment. We also had to continue diving into my childhood.

You know something, Angelina? After so many sessions with Sergio, I don't feel so bad about being a pathological liar or an occasional kleptomaniac or bipolar or an anxiety-attack sufferer or immoderately fond of shopping. I admire people like you who get involved in humanitarianism, who care about humanity. I like that you visit refugees in Lebanon or direct movies. I think I've matured a bit and I appreciate generosity, talent, solidarity. I'm not as frivolous as you think, really. I'm sure this blog have soiled your opinion of me; I wish it didn't.

***

Finally, some good news, Angelina! Emilio was right and the judge dismissed Ramona's family's lawsuit against the Valdeluz Residence. It was my word against Desiré's, who'd claimed that she saw me in the hallway with the old lady's bracelet sticking out of my pocket. The judge said that the flash of gold that Desiré said she saw wasn't solid enough evidence to convict me of stealing Ramona Pérez Lastra's bracelet. I understood that taking a piece of jewelry from a demented old woman wasn't exactly commendable, but I didn't feel guilty. Her family deserved it—they hadn't visited her since she was first admitted to Valdeluz, and the poor thing was suffering too much neglect to have enjoyed that bracelet or any of her other jewelry.

Mom was overjoyed to learn that I'd gotten off scott-free and immediately got back to lobbying me to use the money from my inheritance for the down payment on an apartment. She even offered to help me pay the mortgage.

***

To celebrate my legal victory, on Sunday Mom and I invited Marta to lunch. Mom was very happy. Cesar arrived first—it was his weekend off, when his kids were staying with his ex-wife. I was wearing a new emerald blouse I'd just bought, the same shade you wore to the Golden Globes in 2011.

Marta came late like always, for the attention. We all turned to her as she made her way in, watching her mov with an unself-conscious resolve, like a palm tree in summer. As we sat down to eat Mom's inevitable Spanish omelet, she reminded me again of a vacation advertisement far away from our neighborhood and the northeast-facing living room that constituted my mother's only property.

She wore her glasses carelessly hooped over her wavy hair. The air carried a warm, sweet perfume. I was in high mode, thinking of Bruno and what his voice would be like up close, warm, husky, sometimes teasing.

Marta moved, helping Mom, around our dining room as if on a stage, her body trimming at every turn. They were both placing the food on top of the resin table, but it was too inelegant for her.

"I always like to use a tablecloth."

"Don't worry, it's fine like this."

She always liked the sorts of details that David described as petit bourgeois. I took another bite from my plate.

"If you keep this up, the next time you go shopping you'll have to look in the plus-size section."

From time to time she had these moments of cruelty. If a look could kill, I would have struck down my mother that very second.

"Angelina is going to own an apartment," she shouted later. Whenever she was happy, her voice took on a shrill tone of triumph.

"For God's sake!" I protested. "Mom, haven't you heard about subprime mortgages?"

It was useless—she had it all figured out. A 25,000-euro down payment, she could help me with that and I'd only have to take care of the monthly payments. All night it was impossible to change her mind—or the subject.

Suddenly, out of the blue, mom said something about how cute Marta was and told me that I should start exercising more and join a gym, now that I could afford it.

I ignored the suggestion and asked Marta to take a walk with me. César was going to sleep over that night—I didn't even want to think about the racket he and Mom would make. They played sexy music and everything.

I'd spent the rest of the evening thinking about Bruno.

The next day, I decided to skip taking the pills that my shrink had prescribed. Partly because they made me feel crappy, and also because the package insert made it sound like the possible side effects were worse than the disease they were supposed to cure. Anyway, I figured the best thing to do was to declare myself incurable and embrace my dysfunction—it made me more original, more interesting.

***

It was a dry and hot summer in Madrid. I spent most of the day at home with the blinds down, surfing the internet, thinking about how to seduce Bruno, terrified and excited about our meeting. For the first time I liked my job, if that's what you can call what I was doing on Matching Friends: playing different characters at the same time, dressing up, playing out the fantasies of virtual and anonymous lovers. All the while I never stopped thinking about Bruno for a single minute. Mom, always eager to nag me, complained that I spent too much time in front of the computer. Now that I finally had some money, why didn't I leave the house?

I stopped going to the psychiatrist. It was an easy decision. When I told him at our last session that I didn't plan to come back, Sergio focused his floating attention and glared at me.

"But you haven't made the payment yet!"

I took full responsibility. I didn't want to see a doctor, that was all.

When I got back to the apartment, I had a message from Bruno. "Coffee tomorrow? Just us, for real, in person—any coffee shop you want." I spent the day thinking about how to respond. I hated always giving him the runaround just because I was scared to show him the real me. I sensed that my excuses were making him more and more interested in me, but I knew this couldn't go on forever.

I found a good excuse to delay meeting Bruno: I told him that tomorrow I was planning to go boating with some friends in Turkey. I'd just seen something on TV about Istanbul, one of the world's most beautiful cities. I had promised my friends I'd go and now I couldn't say no.

I Googled photos of Istanbul and, over the next two weeks, posted three of them on Facebook: one of Istiklal Street, one of the Bosphorus Strait, and a third of a mosque with pointed minarets at sunset. "Leave something for our walkabout," Bruno messaged me, disappointed.

He felt so close to me, just a click away, but at the same time there was something painfully inaccessible about him. The dissonance plunged me into a state of permanent anxiety. One of the rules of virtual relationships is to not get hung up on any one user. I felt short of breath.

***

Mom went to Malaga with Cesar for a few days, leaving me alone to concentrate on my work on Matching Friends. In August, lots of people were summering in Madrid without their families, and there were more clients than ever. Apparently, the solitude was conducive to virtual sex.

Chapter 19
Winged Seeds

Thank you Mario. But our princess is in another castle!

SUPER MARIO BROS

By September, my main concern was how to avoid a real meeting with Bruno, who was still insisting to see me. One afternoon, while I was cooking up a new excuse to give my virtual admirer, I got a call. It was the nurse from the gynecologist's office where I'd just gone for a routine check-up.

"You need to come to the hospital tomorrow," she said. "We'd like to redo one of your tests."

"Why?" I asked. "Is something wrong?"

"I don't know anything. The doctor can tell you more."

Not to bore you, Angelina, but that week I was diagnosed with breast cancer that had spread to my uterus. It was already fairly advanced. I realized that there were worse things than having two policemen show up at your door.

***

Two weeks later I had my surgery. Remember how I started this blog by telling you that David had come to see me at the hospital? A week after that, I Vanesa came too.

"Good morning, Angelina," she said. "How are you feeling?"

"Better now," I said. "Should be out of here in a couple days."

"That's great! Honestly, you look amazing."

"It my face serum. Very moisturizing."

There was silence.

"I'm sure you'll recover in no time," Vanesa assured me. "I have a few friends who have gone through the same thing and already forgotten all about it."

"Right," I answered. "Everyone tells me the same thing. Things like 'Medicine has come a long way in this' or 'Just focus on getting well as soon as possible.' And just before they say goodbye: 'What do you need? Do you want me to get you anything?'"

Vanessa shyly approached my bed with a package.

"I brought you a gift, just a silly little thing."

"Thank you."

"I can open it for you if you want. Don't want to mess up your IV."

It was one of those baskets with lotions and creams and perfumes, wrapped in cellophane and tied with a bow.

I wanted her to leave. I looked at my phone to check the time.

"While you're on your phone, you can follow me on Instagram. I've been following you for a long time, reading everything you post about celebrities and stuff."

I nodded, though I had no intention of going to her profile.

"How many followers do you have on Instagram?" she asked.

"Oh, I don't know," I laughed. "I haven't counted."

"I have 50,000," she said.

"Damn girl!"

David's visit had left me indifferent; Vanesa's got on my nerves. I couldn't stand her! The days of our friendship felt so far in the past. I finally realized the magnitude of the rift between us, and I wanted her out of my life. I didn't even care if she and David were still seeing each other. She spoke to me as if she was excusing herself, afraid that I was going to get angry and insult her. Something had settled in her, had taken shape in the luminous darkness of her hair, the girl from the shampoo commercial.

"I hope you're not still mad at me," she said.

"Oh, no! What you do in your private life is none of my business."

I really did feel that way. It was hilarious to remember that at one point I'd thought about killing myself over David. Now I couldn't care less about the two of them—I just didn't want them to visit me anymore.

David was just a pretentious, posh wannabe, an incessant social climber, always bragging about his ridiculous jobs. And as for Vanessa, I despised her vanity, her preening, her stupid Instagram account and how she fell for any available man at the drop of a hat. She wanted to be some sort of femme fatale, with rich and powerful men falling at her feet, a cross between Marilyn Monroe and Coco Chanel. If people like the two of them would think that they are likely to obtain very few of the things they have aspired to throughout their lives and that after their death they will fall into absolute oblivion, just like those branches that are cut by the wind and go to the garbage, they would abandon that imbecilic smile of smugness.

"I'll head out soon—I don't want to be a bother," Vanesa said.

"You're no bother," I lied. "On the contrary—stay as long as you want."

I was beginning to understand the advantages of being fake as fuck.

"I have to leave at eight anyway," she said.

She seemed nervous. I imagined that she was meeting David.

"Give my regards to your mother," she said as she left.

Mom was somewhere off with Cesar, as usual.

"I'll be sure to do that."

My last sentence resonated within me with an elegant and disdainful intonation. I was beginning to learn how to behave.

When Vanessa left, I looked her up on Facebook. Her profile was crammed with photos, all the same, groups of smiling girl-friends with their thumbs up in a pathetic gesture of triumph. David's profile—it seemed he had unblocked me—was even worse. He posted stupid shit like "Happy Monday" and "Sweet dreams." I thought that both of them in their respective virtual *alter egos* gave the full measure of their imbecility.

***

The oncologist visited me this morning, Angelina, and told me that the surgery went very well and that I have a good chance of survival. In a few days, if I continue to improve, I'll be discharged. Then I'll have to start chemo, but the doctor says I'll handle it just fine. While I've been recovering at the hospital, I've had enough strength to open up my laptop and write a weekly blog post. Bruno kept insisting that we meet, so I wrote him and said that I had something to tell him: I was married, and I was too afraid to tell him until now. That's why I'd been delaying our date; my husband had been sick for some time and I'd been taking care of him. Why was I lying? I wanted to keep my illness under wraps, wanted to keep up that colorful, happy image of my life. Wanted to be the girl from the shampoo commercial.

Bruno was upset to learn that I was in fact taken. Then he told me that he had a girlfriend, but was thinking of dumping her, though he didn't know how. I was relieved to think that for the moment I had a good excuse not to see him in person; I even helped him brainstorm how to break up with her. Later, I would regret not telling him about my surgery and chemo. If I wanted to be with him, if we wanted to finally go on our walkabout, the logical thing to do was to just tell the truth, get everything out in the open. But I'm weak, insecure. I always need to sugarcoat reality.

***

Mom came to pick me up from the hospital today. She shot me a little forced smiled as she helped me pack my suitcase. Even Dad came to congratulate me on my return home. We all had dinner together, takeout washed down with a bottle of sparkling wine, just for the occasion. But mom had another surprise up her sleeve. She said she was going to give me 10,000 euros from her savings, which, combined with what Dad would give me from his retirement fund, and my money from Don Ramiro, would make me the owner of a 100 square-meter apartment when I finished paying the mortgage in 20 years' time. When she showed me the floor plan, I remembered the ranch that David and I would never live in. Maybe it was better that it had disappeared from my life, from the plans David and I made. From everywhere, except from that little corner of my subconscious.

Chapter 20
No Organ Was Formed to Give Pain

Hope is what makes us stronger. It is the reason we are here. It's what we fight for when all else is lost.

PANDOR

Angelina, I haven't been able to write a blog post for a long time. Chemo has left me too tired and weak, but a couple of weeks ago I started to feel better and I'm starting to get back to life as usual. The first thing I did was to go to El Corte Inglés. So far this year I have been very frugal with my shopping, and the money from Don Ramiro, except for what I had to give for the down payment on the apartment, remains untouched. Rummaging through El Corte Inglés like a kid in a candy store, I felt cured. Contained within these walls was a world in which happiness was found in the simplest of moments: picking out a rare find from a big pile, watching the cashier delicately take my card and return it with a smile. My comfort zone, my happy place, where everything has a reason for being. Nowadays, happiness and possession are synonyms. If I hadn't ended up working on dating sites, I would have liked to be a personal shopper, taking millionaires on shopping sprees around the world.

***

Let me tell you a little more about Bruno. His last name is Fedragotti because his grandfather is Italian. He studied architecture, and soon he will have his own studio. He is richer and better-looking than me. He is also more cultured—he only likes good movies, good music, good books. I get all my culture from the internet, the video games David showed me, glossy magazines and self-help books and Wikipedia articles.

Bruno says I stimulate him. He calls me his muse, his inspiration. We're both ready to take the leap and have a real relationship. The question is when. I'm putting it off, but I know it's coming. Strange as it sounds, we's starting to see a real future together. He finds my job as a metadata manager—though he doesn't have all the details about what that actually means—to be fun and modern.

A la mode, he called it. He said that means trendy in French; he speaks very good French.

I wouldn't mind renting out my new apartment and going to live with him in Milan or London or Rome. If everything goes well and we end up becoming a couple, of course. I love learning languages, and the advantage of a job like mine is that I can do it from anywhere.

We're starting to trust each other more and more, and I think we both fantasize about our future, like fiancées looking forward to their wedding date. He told me that he's already the father of two children, a boy and a girl, both from his first marriage, and he doesn't want to have any more children. I told him that I don't like children, so I don't mind not having any of my own. Bruno's children, fortunately, live with their mother. She and my boyfriend—I'm already calling him that, secretly—got divorced five years ago.

***

When I opened my laptop, there was a message waiting for me from an anonymous user: "I know where you live and I'm going to find you". There was no signature. I read it again before video chatting Bruno.

"Angelina, my dear, what a pleasant surprise!" he answered. "I wasn't expecting you at this hour."

"I'm really scared. I think someone is stalking me."

I read the message to him.

"Why don't I come over so you won't be alone?"

"That's really kind of you, Bruno, but today Mom and César are here. He's staying over this weekend."

"I don't want you to feel afraid. Angie, as long as I'm with you, nothing will happen to you. We'll track down whoever is doing this and report them. The first thing you have to do is block the account; second, collect evidence, we'll take care of that; and third, ask for help—that's what I'm here for. For now, look up the info for this account called Stop Haters. They can help you."

"I feel better already."

"Listen, Angelina, I'm going to leave my cell phone on all night. Can call me anytime, doesn't matter if it's late. I want you to feel safe."

I tried calling the support desk for Matching Friends. No one answered the phone, so I sent an e-mail explaining that I wanted to delete my account. It must take a few hours for them to delete your account because the stalker kept contacting me. Then I changed my email and Instagram passwords.

I reached out to Stop Haters and searched for more organizations that could help me. Their websites informed me that internet stalking happens mostly to minors or women between the ages of 25 and 35. I am not in that bracket.

Until now, I used to spend six hours a day working on Matching Friends, mostly during peak hours: from twelve to three in the morning and from five to eight in the evening. Sometimes I would take weekends off to talk to Bruno, and because I thought that when I was with him we would go out with friends and I wouldn't be sitting around every Friday and Saturday night in front of a computer.

Almost all my clients operated under pseudonyms, but the site admins knew their identities and credit card numbers. The site attracted all kinds of people: AIDS patients, men impotent despite Viagra, women who hated their bodies, bored housewives seeking adventure. Starting at midnight, from Monday to Thursday, when I started my session, I chatted and Zoomed and sent photos and videos and, above all, tried to anticipate and fulfill my clients' fantasies. By 3AM, I logged off and went to sleep.

My clients gave me lots of nicknames, mostly relating to animals: I was a sexy little wolf, a sexy little panther, a sexy little crocodile, a sexy little tiger, a sexy little dove. I always had to be careful, dependable, because my clients could be quite erratic: if they didn't find me desirable even more a moment they would immediately look for new girls.

Angelina, now I want to put an end to all of it and start a new life.

I deactivated my Instagram account. I took a last look at my content—beauty tutorials, self-care tips, celebrity news—and said goodbye to my followers. From now on, the only thing that matters to me is taking that *walkabout,* entering the next stage of my life with Bruno by my side.

I texted him that night before I went to sleep. I had washed my hair and put on special underwear. I remember Sharon Stone said in an interview once that when she had an important work meeting, she always wore stockings and garter belt. Only she knew what she was wearing under her skirt, but it was enough. You can notice something without having to see it. By the way, Angelina, I recently this other thing about Sharon Stone that I thought was really funny. I guess she had signed up for a Bumble account under her real name, and a bunch of users reported her account as fake. Bumble thought it was fake too—like, what would Sharon Stone be doing on *Bumble*?—and suspended her, until she finally tweeted about it. "Don't exclude me from the hive," she wrote underneath a screenshot of her suspended account.

Bruno was FaceTiming me.

"Good evening, my little dove. Are you feeling any better?"

-Yes, I followed all your advice and deleted all my social media," I said. I paused. "Wait did you just call me your little dove? You've never called me that before."

Only my Matching Friends clients called me that. I didn't want him to—it reminded me of a chapter of my life that now considered closed.

"If you don't like it, I'll never call you that again, Angie, my Marcelo Usera's Scheherazade. How's that?"

"Yes, better."

"Tomorrow we'll file a police report," he said.

I wasn't keen on calling the police; I was still recovering from the last time they paid me a visit.

We kept FaceTiming and when Bruno leaned toward the camera and I felt him caress me with his blue-eyed gaze, I knew that we'd be taking our walkabout soon.

Chapter 21
The Final Extinction

Outside the mercury was falling fast. It was colder
than the devil's heartland and ice slides were
raining down as if the sky was ready to fall.

MAX PAYNE

With Marta's help, I finally bought an apartment of my own. I was officially independent, freed from an endless adolescence spent in the shadow of my mother. The apartment was in Usera in front of Pradolongo Park, which I could see from my bedroom window. I went furniture-shopping at IKEA and Mom, as always, insisted on accompanying me. I already had the essentials for the first few days. My first night in the new apartment, I slept in the master bedroom—yes, this place has *two* bedrooms. In the distance I could see a tall cypress tree that looked like the one in an Italian villa I'd seen on some TV show, I can't remember the name. The next day Marta would go to help me with the rest of the move. She had found a secretarial job with a company based in London, and in a month she was going to move there. She encouraged me to come and visit her.

I had placed my old Fancy Nancy doll on a shelf in my room. It used to be Lara's. Marta told me that it was old and tacky and I should just throw it away. But I didn't. I think that I'm sentimental deep down, and maybe a bit tacky too. The thing is, I liked to look at Fancy Nancy while I was talking to you, Angelina, even though ours has always been a one-sided conversation.

***

The first time Mom came over and saw Fancy Nancy, she looked frightened, like she had seen a snake.

"I found it when I was moving," I said. "I thought I'd keep it, something to remember Lara by."

When she left, I grabbed a yogurt and some fruit from the fridge and started writing a script for my session that night on Matching Friends. Sometimes, I would help myself with note cards like politicians do for their speeches. As I looked at the old doll sitting on my shelf, I was momentarily distracted and the letters on my screen began to jumble and when I hit the delete key to erase all the mistakes and rewrite everything, my computer went crazy—the cursor took on a mind of its own, zigzagging across the screen and deleting everything I'd written. The computer would no longer accept any command. I managed to disconnect it and after a few minutes it crashed, after sending the fruits of my labor, my scripts, which I thought were brilliant, straight to the trash can. But I didn't care if my scripts were lost because I had nowhere left to share them. I had, however, realized how much I liked to write.

I had a headache. I crawled into bed determined to take a short nap. Fancy Nancy was staring at me from the bookshelf, an unwelcome witness to my past. I closed my eyes: it was a summer day like this one…

***

My oncologist had told me I had a good chance of being completely cured, of living a good life. Lara did not get that. Dying at the age of five would be a great tragedy if its protagonist were aware, at least for a few minutes, of what it means. But the death of children is sadder and sweeter: in the old days, when children died they used to put the drawing of an angel in their obituary. Lara will never know jealousy or desire, will never experience doubts or small pleasures. Nor will she ever know the sweetest moments that life has to offer: a picnic in the countryside, an afternoon tryst in an abandoned shack, a friend who says that your face reminds her of Angelina Jolie's. Nor will she know the fear of getting sick again, of getting too sick, of not being liked enough by someone who is only an image and a name, maybe a fake image and a fake name, but someone once said, I think a character from one of David's video games, that every truth has some lie in it and every lie some truth in it.

I closed my eyes, desperate doze off for a while wrapped in this sweet twilight. Lara and I were in our room, alone. It must have been nap time. Dad and Mom had gone out and Mad told me before she left: "You have to take care of Lara, Mari Pili, you're the oldest." I see mom kissing us goodbye and Lara in bed hugging her new doll, her angelic curls grazing her cheeks.

I could hear the background noise of the city, but it sounded like the sea to me, a sea that reached the curtain that covered the window opening. Lara was tossing and turning in her bed, she wouldn't let me sleep... I heard her get up, but I didn't want to move, I wanted to stay exactly where I was, as if I were sunbathing on a beach. I heard the noise of a chair dragging across the hardwood floor, but I didn't raise my head to look, just opened my eyes a little. The chair was already in front of the window, she was holding her doll in her other hand. I watched through my half-closed eyelids. I knew what she was going to do, but some weight prevented me from moving. I didn't call to her, I didn't get up, I didn't approach her or take her by the arm, I didn't call mom. I didn't do any of that. I just closed my eyes and waited. I waited for what seemed like a very long time with my eyes closed. You can't ask of children what you ask of adults. I just wanted to close my eyes, not see anything, not think about anything, stay still; to wrap myself in that summer gloom like a blue and gray quilt, a quilt that weighed me down, wouldn't let me speak or move. I just wanted to stay there and for time to stop, for mom and dad to never come home and start screaming, which is what happened when they saw the window open and that Lara was not in her little bed. On the floor, next to the chair, there was only her doll.

"Did your parents ever talk to you about the accident?" Sergio asked me on the first day of our therapy.

"No, they didn't want to talk about it."

"Do you think this has something to do with your not liking children?"

"No, nothing to do with it. I just don't like taking care of kids, that's all."

"Were there any incidents during your time as a nanny?"

"No. None. Nothing noteworthy ever happened."

Recalling my conversation with Sergio, that memory, buried for so many years, had suddenly found its way into the summer gloom of my new apartment. Like lightning through the clouds.

I got out of bed. Fancy Nancy was still on her shelf, half slumped to the right, between an old encyclopedia and some useless CDs that I had forgotten to throw away.

Marta is right, I thought. *Nancy's corny. I'll toss her out the window.*

The blinds in my new house are automatic, they open and close with a remote control. Nothing like the grass blinds of my childhood.

Finally, I threw the doll in the trash; I didn't want it to fall on the head of some passerby. That was no way to inaugurate my stay in this new home. My freshly painted bedroom seemed cleaner and bigger without her.

Chapter 22
Orchid Sterility

"What are you worried about?"
"Death, I want to live longer."

BLADE RUNNER

Mom is coming to see me again; she wants to see how everything's turned out. She seems to think that the apartment is hers, that she's young again and starting a new life. When she comes into my room and looks at the shelf where Fancy Nancy used to be, I think I see a look of relief in her eyes.

She says he likes the apartment very much, especially the view of the cypress tree and the park out the window.

I have to get used to that word, *window*. Window. Saying the word naturally, like I have nothing to hide. Now, with furniture, the apartment looks different. I'm happy to live here, in a space that's just for me. I'll admit that Mom was right about my buying this place. When I sit down at my computer, a headline catches my attention: "Vanesa Moreno Announces Upcoming Wedding to Video Game Producer David Alonso." There's a link to her website where she gives all the details: the location (a seaside hotel in Oporto); her custom-made dress; her registry, filled with luxury items like the ones she posts about...

***

I wrote another blog post today. It may be the last one, Angelina. I think I'm done with this blog. Of course, I will remain your fan and keep following you. By the way, Angelina, I forgot to tell you: Bruno confessed to me that he lied. He's not an architect but a draftsman, and he has no plans to ever leave Spain. Honestly, it didn't bother me that his profile was less than accurate. Come to think of it, what would a girl like me even do in Milan or London or Paris—way too sophisticated for my blood! I prefer a less glamorous life than one spent accompanying him at architecture conferences or dining at fancy restaurants with his important clients, like I'd imagined. I confessed to him too, about my cancer and my bad experience with David, that I've never been married and have a new apartment in my old neighborhood. The only thing that hasn't changed is our plans for the walkabout.

***

Bruno and I finally got to meet. I went to the hairdresser's right before. My hair was really short because of chemo, but the stylist *blow-dried* the ends. It looked great and made me look younger. I wore an off-white skirt and burgundy jacket that Don Ramiro bought me at Yves Saint Laurent. Between the flattering cut of the jacket and the fact that I'd followed instructions of my most recent diet to the letter, the result was spectacular. Marta, who had come to say goodbye before her flight to London, hyped me up and assured me repeatedly that everything was going to be fine with Bruno.

We had arranged to meet at seven in the evening at my new apartment. On the bar cart I'd just bought at IKEA, I placed a bottle of gin and a bottle of whiskey *alongside* cans of tonic and Coca-Cola. I checked the time on my phone: it was a quarter past seven. He was running a little late. At half past seven I called him, but it went to voicemail. I texted him. At eight o'clock I checked my texts. Nothing. My messages to him were still unread. I called him again, straight to voicemail. I made myself a gin and tonic. I had set out some chips and nuts and sliced ham. I ate two slices of ham, then poured myself another gin. At nine o'clock I drank what was left of the bottle. I got up to close the windows, which I'd left open to show off the view of the park , and grabbed a handful of chips and a handful of nuts. At ten o'clock I checked my texts one more time. My message to him was still unread. I turned off the low light bulbs, which I'd bought because I thought they were more flattering and created an atmosphere of intimacy. I wandered around my new apartment for a while. I read a chapter from one of my self-help books, *How to Make Good Things Happen to You.* The title seemed a bit overconfident, though very appealing—who doesn't want good things to happen to them?

At midnight I went to bed.

Chapter 23
Doubtful Species

Bruno just sent me the photos of the hospital where his father was admitted the night we were supposed to meet; a heart attack. The IV climbs up the bed like a snake until it arrives at his arm. In the next photo they are both posing, his father sitting up a little, Bruno smiling and putting his arm around his neck.

"It was a hellish night—the ambulance, the patience intake, you can't imagine the stress! But he's better now. They say there's still some risk, especially these first two days. Forgive me for not letting you know.

"Of course, I completely understand."

"Are still afraid, Angie?"

"A little bit. Someone knows where I live."

I feel better knowing that soon Bruno will be with me.

***

Hi, Angelina, I haven't written in this blog for a long time. The truth is that I've been neglecting you a little. But came to mind again today. Leafing through old magazines, I reread an article about your divorce with Brad. I wish I could have been there to support you through that difficult time. When I saw you, Angelina, in those old photos, dressed in black, skeletal, I understood how fragile the line is between illness and health, ugliness and beauty, desire and disgust, failure and success. But you'll always be my idol.

Everyone, no matter how successful, has trauma, big or small. People associate Hollywood with the excesses of drugs, alcohol, infidelity, but it's just the same as everywhere else, only in my neighborhood it's less glamorous. I don't care about the gossip—that Brad was sad to lose you, that you wanted to leave Hollywood to devote yourself to being a mother and a humanitarian, that you might not even get custody of your kids. It's not these salacious rumors that keep me interested in you. That's why I didn't even go to see the movie that Brad was in with the actress with whom people said he'd cheated on you. They advertised the movie heavily, hyping up the chemistry between Brad and his costar. I know all the tricks of marketing, I learned them when I worked on dating sites. Love and marketing are similar. Both require imagination, seduction, desire.

***

Right now I am happy to tell you, Angelina, that I feel calm and happy. There's been no sign of the internet stalker in a while. I'm no longer afraid. And I've decided on my new career path—I am going study to be an esthetician and inherit my mother's clients so that she can retire. I already know so much about beauty, so I don't think the training should be too hard for me.

***

Angelina, today I want to say goodbye to you. But first I want you to know something: at last, at last, at last I'm going to meet Bruno! I am no longer a solitary orchid—I'm a pollinated flower. I feel my body hatching, like a seed ripened in the sun, about to explode in the summer heat.

I need to see him, smell his scent and, above all, feel the reality of him. Bruno, in my imagination, smells of leather, horses, cologne, the country. Like a man. How *do* men smell? God I'm so anxious, I'm a carnivorous plant, I want to trap him between my petals. Who was that asshole who called me frigid?

Tomorrow, it will be tomorrow, Angelina. It may be a mistake. But it had to happen sometime, and for me—maybe because of my frigid streak that Sergio was telling me about—there is nothing more erotic than absence. The waiting only fuels my desire and reality rarely meets my expectations. I know that better than anyone.

I've been thinking, Angelina, and don't be angry, that I'd like to go by Mari Pili again, or just Pilar. I admire you, just as I've always admired you, but I think it's time for me to rediscover my true identity, to accept my reality, as my mother tells me. She is still with Cesar, sitll acting like an old married couple. He finally got divorced and they're threatening to move in together.

Goodbye, dear Angelina, je vous souhaite aussi beaucoup de bonheur. See? I've already learned some French. I know you speak it too, you're teaching it to your kids. I've used it with some clients. I'm not as dumb as I look, but I've already told you that.

Dear Angelina, maybe we'll see each other one day, in Hollywood or in Madrid.

Yours forever,

Pilar

This blog and Angelina's dating profile were extracted from her computer by the police, after searching her home to ascertain her whereabouts. A week after writing her final blog post, her mother, María Peinado, sixty-five years old, divorced, a masseuse and beautician, went to her local police station, 35 Marcelo Usera Street, to report her daughter's disappearance. The mother stated that she had been trying unsuccessfully to contact her for three days. One of her neighbors stated that he had last seen her leaving the house with a large bag, dressed as if she was going to a party, at seven o'clock in the evening, three days before the police filed the report of her disappearance.

Madrid, June 15, 2022